Christian Melville

Mrs. Oliphant

Alpha Editions

This edition published in 2024

ISBN : 9789367241882

Design and Setting By
Alpha Editions
www.alphaedis.com
Email - info@alphaedis.com

As per information held with us this book is in Public Domain.
This book is a reproduction of an important historical work. Alpha Editions uses the best technology to reproduce historical work in the same manner it was first published to preserve its original nature. Any marks or number seen are left intentionally to preserve its true form.

Contents

EPOCH I. ....- 1 -
CHAPTER I. ....- 2 -
CHAPTER II. ....- 6 -
CHAPTER III. ....- 9 -
EPOCH II. ....- 13 -
CHAPTER I. ....- 14 -
CHAPTER II. ....- 19 -
EPOCH III. ....- 25 -
CHAPTER I. ....- 26 -
CHAPTER II. ....- 32 -
EPOCH IV. ....- 38 -
CHAPTER I. ....- 39 -
CHAPTER II. ....- 43 -
CHAPTER III. ....- 48 -
CHAPTER IV. ....- 56 -
EPOCH V ....- 63 -
CHAPTER I. ....- 64 -
CHAPTER II. ....- 72 -
CHAPTER III. ....- 80 -

EPOCH I.

'Tis beautiful to see the holy might
Of a strong spirit, dedicate to God,
'Tis beautiful to mark the uplifted light,
In vigorous hands pointing the heavenward road,
Continuing steadfast in the noble strife,
Through the world's dimness shining strong and free;
But fairer still, 'mid quiet household life,
A calm sad chastened spirit praising Thee!
Thee! oh, our Father! from whose hands its thread
Of fate hath run in darkness. Grief's wide veil
Mantling its youthful days—and o'er its head,
The weeping cloud of fear, while yet its pale
And gentle face is radiant with the faith,
That clings although thou smite, nor quits its hold with Death.

CHAPTER I.

But deep this truth impress'd my mind—
Thro' all his works abroad,
The heart benevolent and kind
The most resembles God.—BURNS.

THE sun had set upon the last evening of a cold and bleak December, and from the frosty sky, a few stars looked down upon the crowded streets of one of the largest towns in England; a motley scene, in which the actors, both gay and sorrowful, went whirling and winding onwards, altogether unconscious of other scrutiny than from the busy eyes of their fellows. It was still early, and the whole scrambling restless world of the great town was astir, pouring out its many-tongued din over the cheerful pavements, bright with the light from its open shops and warehouses, and throwing its wide stream, in ceaseless and ever-spreading volumes, through street and lane and alley. Working men were hastening homewards, with baskets of tools slung over their stalwart shoulders, and empty pitchers dangling "at the cold finger's end." Dignified merchants, lean men of arts and letters, spruce commercial gentlemen, blended among each other like ripples in a river. Here there was an eddy, where the stream, branching out, swept off in another direction; there a whirlpool, where the flood pouring in, from a world of converging ways, involved itself for a moment in mazy bewilderment, before it found its purposed channel once more: but everywhere there was the same full and incessant flow, bearing in its broad bosom the unfailing concomitants of loud-voiced mirth and secret misery, of anger and of peacefulness, poverty and wealth, apathy and ambition, which marked its stream for human.

It is not with these many-voiced brilliant streets we have to do to-night, but with a household in one of them. A very quiet house you may see it is, though not a gloomy one, for light is shining from the yet uncurtained windows, pleasant thoughtful cheering fire-light, and the room has about it the indefinable comfort and brightness of home. It has at present but one occupant, and she—there is nothing about her appearance at all extraordinary—she is not very young—not less than thirty summers have past over those grave and thoughtful features, and given experience to the quiet intelligence of those clear eyes—nor beautiful, though those who knew it, loved to look upon her face, and thought there was there something higher than beauty. You would not think, to see her now, how blithe her nature was, and how unusual this sadness; but she *is* sorrowful to-night. It may be, that in her cheerful out-goings and in-comings, she has not time to indulge in any sad recollections, but that they have overcome her, in such a quiet evening hour as this. The shadows are gathering thicker and deeper, and the windows of neighbouring houses are all bright, but this room retains its twilight still. Its solitary tenant leans her head upon her hand, and gazes into the vacant air, as though she sought for some retiring figure and found it not. And why may she not be sad? She is a Christian thoughtful and pure-minded, and the last hours of another year are wearing themselves away, and is there no food for sadness here?

But there are voices that breathe no sorrow nor sadness coming in through the half-open door. There is one, a sweet indefinite tone, which speaks half of childhood, and half of graver years; there is boisterous rejoicing and obstreperous boyishness in another, and there is a grave voice, as joyful, but deep and quiet; and, here they come, each one more mirthful than the other. There is a sprightly girl of some fifteen summers, a youth her proud superior by two undoubted twelvemonths, and an elder brother, whose maturer features bear a yet more striking resemblance to the silent sister, the eldest of them all, about whose ears a storm of fun and reproof comes rattling down.

"Christian had no time!" says the sage wisdom of seventeen; "yet here is grave Christian dreaming away her hours in the dim fire-light."

"You were too busy, Christian, to go out with me," remonstrates little Mary—for the endearing caressing epithet "little," though often protested against, was still in use in the household—"and you are doing nothing now."

But Christian only smiles: strange it seems, that Christian should smile so sadly!

Now the youthful tongues are loosed. They have been on an important visit: to-morrow is to see that grave and blushing brother the master of another house, and that house has this night been subjected to the admiration and criticism of the younger members of the family, and all they have seen and wondered at must needs be told now for Christian's information; but the elder sister listens with vacant inattentive ear, and irresponsive eye, until Robert grows indignant, and protests with boyish fervour, that "It's a shame for her to be so grave and sad, and James going to be married to-morrow!" James, the bridegroom, does not however seem to think so, for he checks his youthful brother, and bends over Christian tenderly, and Christian's eyes grow full, and tears hang on the long lashes. What can make Christian so sad? Let us go with her to her chamber, and we shall see.

It is a quiet airy pleasant room, rich enough to please even an Oxford scholar of the olden time, for there are more than "twenty books clothed in black and red" within its restricted space. There is one windowed corner, at which, in the summer time, the setting sun streams in, and for this cause Christian has chosen it, as the depository of her treasures. There is a portrait hanging on the wall; a mild apostolic face, with rare benignity in its pensive smile, and genius stamped upon its pale and spiritual forehead: too pale, alas! and spiritual; for the first glance tells you, that the original can no longer be in the land of the living. A little table stands below it, covered with books—a few old volumes worthy to be laid beneath the word of truth—and there too lies a Bible. It has a name upon it, and a far-past date, and its pages tell of careful perusal, and its margin is rich with written comments, and brief, yet clear, and forcible remarks. Below the name, a trembling hand has marked another date—you can see it is this day five years—and a text, "Blessed are the dead who die in the Lord, for they have entered into their rest, and their works do follow them." The faltering hand was that of Christian Melville, and thus you have the story of her sadness. This place is the favourite sanctuary of that subdued and chastened spirit; a holy trysting-place, that has been filled often with a presence greater than that of earthly king or lord, and Christian is always happy here, even though—yea, verily, because—she does sit among these relics of a bygone time, of youthful hopes and expectations which long ago have come to an end and passed away for ever.

But Christian has other duties now. A heavier step has entered the dwelling, and she goes calm and cheerful again, and hastens to take her seat at the merry table, where the father of the family now sits; their only parent, for they are motherless. Mr. Melville is a good man. There are none more regular, more exemplary, in the whole ranks of the town's respectability; his pew has never been vacant in the memory of church-going men; his neighbours have not the shadow of an accusation to bring against him; his character is as upright as his bearing; his conscience as pure as his own linen. It has been whispered, that his heart has more affinity to stone than is befitting the heart of a living man; but Mr. Melville is a gentleman of the highest respectability, and doubtless that is a slander. He is of good means, he is just in all his relations, he is courteous, and if he be not pitiful withal, how can so small an omission detract from a character otherwise so unexceptionable? His wife has been dead for two or three years, and he speaks of her, as "his excellent deceased partner." Christian says, her mother had the spirit of an angel, and her memory is yet adored by all the household; but Mr. Melville is a calm person, and does not like raptures. His family consists of five children. Christian—whose history we have already glanced at, summed up in her precious relics—is the eldest; then, there is the bridegroom, James, an excellent well-disposed young man, just about to form a connection after his father's own heart; next in order comes the genius of the family, gay, talented, excitable, generous Halbert, over whose exuberance of heart his correct parent shakes his head ominously. This Halbert is a student, and absent from home at present, so we cannot present him to our readers just now. Robert is the next in order, a blithe careless youth, having beneath his boyish gaiety, however, a good deal of the worldly prudence and calculating foresight of his father and eldest brother; and little Mary, the flower of all, finishes the list. Mary is the feminine and softened counterpart of her genius-brother; there is light flashing and sparkling in her eyes that owns no kindred with the dull settled gleam of the paternal orbs. There is a generous fire and strength in her spirit which shoots far beyond the coolness and discretion of prudent calculating James, and in her school attainments she has already far surpassed Robert—much to the latter's chagrin and annoyance at being beaten by a girl—and these two, Halbert and Mary, are Christian's special care.

It is quite true, that her watchful attention hovers about her cold father in a thousand different ways. It is quite true, that there cannot be a more affectionate sister than Christian to her elder and younger brothers; but little anxiety mingles with her affection for, and care of, them. Their names are not forgotten in her frequent prayers, and her voice is earnest and fervent, and her heart loving, when she craves for them the promised blessings and mercies of the Almighty; but her accents tremble in her supplications when those other names are on her lips, for visions of snares and pitfalls laid for their beloved feet have darkened her foreboding fancy with visions of shipwrecked faith and failing virtue, of ruined hopes and perverted talents, until the very agony of apprehensive love has invested its objects with a higher interest than even that of closest kindred. It is hers to watch over, to lead, to direct, to preserve the purity, to restrain the exuberance of these gifted spirits, and therefore is there a dignity in Christian's eye when she looks on these children of her affections, that beams not from its clear depths at any other time, and an unconscious solemnity in her pleasant voice when her kind and gentle counsel falls upon their ears, that strangers wonder at—for Christian is young—to be so like a mother.

Such is the family of Mr. Melville, of the prosperous firm of Rutherford and Melville, merchants, in the great English town, to whom we beg to introduce our readers.

CHAPTER II.

Yes, the year is growing old,
And his eye is pale and blear'd!
Death, with frosty hand and cold,
Plucks the old man by the beard
Sorely,—sorely!—LONGFELLOW.

IT is New Year's Eve. There is no twilight now in Mr. Melville's cheery parlour, the light is glimmering in the polished furniture, leaping and dancing in the merry eyes that surround it, and even the grave features of the head of the house have relaxed into an unwonted smile. The young people have not forgotten the old Scottish celebration of "Hogmanay," in all its observances, and Christian's stores have been plundered, and James has fled blushing from their raillery, pursued by the glad echo of their ringing laughter. How pleasantly it sounds! the passengers without on the cold pavement linger at the bright window, arrested by its spell; involuntary smiles steal over grave sober faces, as it rings out in its frank youthfulness challenging their sympathy, and younger passers-by echo it with interest in a chorus of their own, and send it on, louder and louder, through the cold brisk air. How merrily it sounds!

And Christian is smiling too, but her smile is like the first April sunbeam, whose fleeting brightness tells of tears at hand. Her thoughts are solemn; this evening is sacred to the dead, whose image floats before her pensive eyes, and whose cherished memory hangs about her inmost heart. She sees the worn and weary frame, so long since laid down in peace, to sleep and be at rest within the bosom of its mother earth. She holds communion with the immortal nature so long since perfected. She is alone amid that mirth, surrounded by mournful remembrances; among *them*, but united to the dead.

But "James is to be married to-morrow!" and there are household preparations to make, and when these are finished the hour has come for their usual evening worship; a pleasant hour at all times to Christian Melville. Her father has chosen his Psalm appropriately this night, and the solemn and simple melody swells up, full and clear, through their quiet habitation.

"Lord, thou hast been our dwelling place
In generations all,
Before thou ever hadst brought forth
The mountains great or small;
Ere ever thou hadst form'd the earth
And all the world abroad,

Ev'n thou from everlasting art
To everlasting, God."

How vivid is the realisation of Christian, as she sings the words of that solemn acknowledgment of God's power and man's dependence, and, in true heartfelt appreciation of the Lord's providential loving-kindness on the closing night of the year, recognises and gives thanks for His great goodness. And there is a quivering aged voice blending with the sweet youthful accents in the song of gratitude; Christian knows right well that it comes from a heart, a very babe's in godly simplicity, which, in the meek confidence of faith, is enabled and privileged to take the inspired words of the Psalmist for its own. It is old Ailie, her dead mother's faithful and trusted servant, and her own humble friend and counsellor. The reading of the Word is past, the voice of supplication has ceased, and, gathering round the warm fireside, they wait the advent of the new year; happily and with cheerfulness wait for it,—*for it*, for the breath of praise and prayer has driven away the gloom from the calm horizon of Christian's gentle spirit, like a cloud before the freshening gale, and the young faces that know no sorrow are shining with the very sunlight of happiness. Robert's eye is on the time-piece, watching its slow fingers as they creep along to midnight, and Mary has clasped Christian's hand in her own, that none may be before her in her joyful greeting, and the father lingers in his seat half disposed to melt into momentary kindness, and half ashamed of the inclination. Twelve! Listen how it peals from a hundred noisy monitors, filling the quiet midnight air with clamour, and followed by a storm of gratulation and good wishes in this cheerful room, and out of doors from so many human tongues, and so often insincere. There is no feigned affection, however, in this little circle; hand clasps hand warmly, and voice responds to voice with genuine heartiness. Even Mr. Melville has foregone his frost, and hurries away that nobody may see him in his molten state, and Christian calls in Ailie and her younger assistants to give and receive the "happy new year." Christian is no niggard in her annual dainties, and she has risen now with her eyes sparkling:

"A happy new year to Halbert!"

There is a glistening look about those cheerful eyes—for they are cheerful now—which shows that their brightness is all the brighter for a tear hovering under the long lashes; and cordially does every voice in the room echo her wish, "A happy new year to Halbert!" if he were only here to give it back!

But the blithe ceremonial is over, the embers are dying on the hearth, and the young eyelids are closed in sleep; why does Christian linger here? The room is dark, save when some expiring flame leaps up in dying energy before it passes away, yet there she bends in silent contemplation, as the dusky red grows darker and darker, and the ashes fall noiselessly upon the hearth. Is she dreaming over the extinguished hopes which she has hid in mournful solitude within her steadfast heart? Is she comparing, in grief's pathetic power of imagery, these decaying embers with the happy prospects, the abundant promise, which Death's cold fingers have quenched? Ah! Christian has gone far back through the dim vistas of memory to a chamber of sorrow; a darkened room, where lies in its unconscious majesty the garment of mortality which a saint has laid aside. In imagination she weeps her tears all over again, but they are sweet and gentle now, for Time's hand is kind, and there is healing in the touch of his rapid fingers; and now that bitterness worse than death has passed away, and Christian rejoices even in the midst of her sadness, for the one she mourns derived his lineage from the highest blood on earth—the household of faith—and Death has carried him home.

CHAPTER III.

Kind messages, that pass from land to land;
Kind letters, that betray the heart's deep history,
In which we feel the pressure of a hand—
One touch of fire,—and all the rest is mystery!
LONGFELLOW.

THE morning of the new year is dawning as brightly as winter morning may, and Christian is up again among her household, preparing for the great event of the day. Mary and Robert are still employed in their personal adornments, and James, waiting for his graver sister, watches the door in terror for their entry; but Christian at last leads the bridegroom away, and bids the merry youthful couple follow, and James will not forget, for many a year of the new life on which he is about to enter, the gentle sisterly counsel which he now receives: how unselfish, how generous she is! His future wife may be a sister in name, but she can never be so in spirit; Christian knows that well, but how sweetly she speaks of her, how warmly she encourages her brother's affection, how gently she leads his thoughts to his new duties, and urges upon him, in admonitory yet tender kindness, their lasting obligation. His home will be a happy one, if he becomes what Christian wishes and presses him to be.

Mr. Melville fancies that there could not, by any chance, be a better arrangement than James's marriage with Elizabeth Rutherford, the only daughter of his wealthy partner; so natural at once, and business-like, for James of course, will just step into the place vacated by his worthy seniors, when their time comes to depart from Exchange and counting-house: a most excellent arrangement; Elizabeth is a pretty girl too, a little gay perhaps, but time will remedy and quiet that. Christian said some foolish thing about the Rutherfords being vain worldly people, but Christian always spoke foolishly on such subjects. There could not have been a better arrangement, and armed with this deliverance of paternal wisdom, James had been a successful wooer and suitor, and gay Elizabeth Rutherford will be Christian's sister to-day.

We leave the wedding, with all its vows, and pomps, and ceremony, to the imagination of the gentle reader. It will suffice to say, that James was married, and that all went off as well and as merrily as is usually the case. But it is now the new year's night and Christian is at home, and there, lying on her own table, at her own corner of the cheerful fireside, lies a prize; "a letter from Halbert!" Christian has thrown herself into a chair, and is busy unfolding the precious document, and little Mary's bright eyes are sparkling over her shoulder; but we must not describe Halbert's epistle, we shall rather give it *in extenso*.

"My dear Christian,

"I have been congratulating myself, that amidst all your multitudinous avocations at this eventful time, the reading of my periodical epistle will be some relief to you, and in benevolent consideration of your overwhelming cares, intend—in spite of your late reproof on my levity, which natheless, dear Christian, is not levity, but *fun*—to fill this, at present unsullied sheet, with as much nonsense as possible. However, I will so far subdue my propensities, as to make my second sentence—concerning, as it does, so very important an event in the family—a serious enough one. I have a feeling about this marriage of James's which I can hardly explain, even to myself; I suppose, because it is the first break in the family, the first introduction of change; and it seems so extraordinary a thing at first, that we, who have lived all our lives together, should be able to form connections nearer and dearer with others, than those which exist among ourselves. I could almost be glad, Christian, that *your* loss—forgive me for speaking of it—will preserve you to us all; and James's choice too rather surprises me! I was not wont to have a very high idea of Elizabeth Rutherford's qualities; I hope, however, for James's sake, that I have been greatly mistaken: I have written him a congratulatory letter. I must confess to you though, that my congratulations would have been much more cordial, had our new sister-in-law come nearer my ideal. You know that I have a very high standard.

"We are enjoying our moment of breathing time very much—we students—in our classical and poetical retreats in the attics of Edinburgh, putting the stores of mental *plenishing*, which have been accumulating on our hands or lying in disorder in our heads for the past months, into their fitting places and order, and preparing the still unfurnished apartments for the reception of more. I suppose you will be thinking, that in one suite at least of these same empty inner rooms, there will be a vast quantity of clearing out required, before the formerly unmolested heterogeneous literary rubbish give place to the fair array of philosophical and theological lore, which must needs supplant it—and so there is. I do assure you, that at this present moment, the clearing out and scouring goes on vigorously. You should see how I turn my old friends out of doors to make way for the flowing full-robed dignity of their stately successors. The toil of study has, however, so much real pleasure mixed with it, after the first drudgery is over, that I don't long very anxiously for its conclusion, though that is drawing near very rapidly. I suppose, if I am spared, I shall be ready to enter upon the work, to which we have so often looked forward, in little more than eighteen months. Well, time is not wont to be a laggard, and I hope when he runs round that length, he will find me better prepared for the duties and labours of my high vocation than I am now. Do you know, Christian, I have had lately a kind of fearful feeling, whenever I think of the future; what is the cause I cannot tell, unless it be one of those presentiments that sometimes—at least so we have heard—overshadow the minds of people who are, or who are about to be, exposed to danger. I am not, you know, in the least; nevertheless, I have not the same pleasure in looking forward that I used to have. I wish you would try and explain this enigma for me.

"I told you lately, you will remember, that I had made a very agreeable acquaintance, in a Mr. Walter Forsyth. I like him better the more I see of him, for he has great natural ability and extraordinary cultivation, united to the most captivating manners. I know you are very impassive to our masculine attractions, yet I hardly think, Christian, you could help being much pleased with him. He is a good deal older than I am, and is moreover of considerably higher station in the world than a student, and therefore I feel his attention to me the more gratifying. I have been at his house several times, and have met a good many of our Edinburgh *savans* there: none of them of the kind though that you would expect me to be associating with; for Forsyth's friends are not exactly of the same character as my future position would require mine to be. Don't think from this that I have got into bad company—just the reverse, I assure you, Christian—they are almost all very accomplished agreeable men, and I like them exceedingly. Forsyth is very liberal in his ways of thinking, perhaps you might think too much so; but he has mixed much with the world, and travelled a great deal, and so has come to look upon all kinds of opinions with indulgence, however much they may differ from his own: altogether, I cannot sum up his good qualities better than by saying, that he is a most fascinating man. I am afraid you will think I am getting very suddenly attached to my friend, but I feel quite sure he deserves it.

"I charge you to remember me, with all fraternal kindness, to our new sister-in-law. I suppose I shall have to beg pardon personally for various bygone affrays, of which I was the provoker long ago, 'when we were bairns.' Tell Mary I am very much afraid she will be following James's example, and that she must positively let me be first, and for yourself, dear Christian, believe me always

"Your very affectionate brother,
"HALBERT MELVILLE."

The first night of the year fell on a happy household. The senior of all, its head, satisfied and self-complacent; his grave and gentle daughter, full of such hopeful and pleasant thoughts as stifled the strange misgivings and forebodings that had sprung up within her when she had read the character of that much esteemed friend, who already seemed to have secured so large a portion of her brother's affection—in Halbert's letter; and the younger pair, as became the evening of so great a holiday, tired out with their rejoicing. The evening closed cheerily around them, and threw its slumberous curtain about every separate resting-place, as though it had a charge over them in their peaceful sleep, and predicted many a sweet awakening and many a prosperous day.

EPOCH II.

Behold the tempter!—to the expectant air
The hoarse-voiced wind whispers its coming dread,
And ancient Ocean from his mighty head
Shakes back the foaming tangles of his hair,
Gathering his strength that giant power to dare,
That chafes to fury all his thousand waves,
And digs in his deep sand unlooked for graves,
Whelming the hapless barks that voyage there.
Fierce is the rage of elemental strife;
Yet who may tell how far exceeds that war
That rends the inner seat of mental life,
Veils the soul's sky—shuts out each guiding star.
The fiercest tempest raging o'er the sea,
But pictures what the might of mental storms may be.

CHAPTER I.

That there is not a God, the fool
Doth in his heart conclude:
They are corrupt, their works are vile;
Not one of them doth good.
*   *   *   *   *
There feared they much; for God is with
The whole race of the just.—PSALM xiv.

ANOTHER December has begun to lower in the dim skies with wintry wildness, to bind the earth with iron fetters, and to cover its surface with its snowy mantle, as we enter for the first time another town, far from that English borough in which we lingered a year ago. An ancient city is this, within whose time-honoured walls the flower and pride of whatever was greatest and noblest in Scotland, has ever been found through long descending ages. Elevated rank, mighty mental ability, eminent piety, the soundest of all theology, the most thorough of all philosophy, and the truest patriotism, have ever been concentrated within its gates. Here men are common, who elsewhere would be great, and the few who do stand out from amid that mass of intellect stand out as towers, and above that vast aggregate of genius and goodness are seen from every mountain in Christendom, from every Pisgah of intellectual vision, whereon thoughtful men do take their stations, as suns amid the stars. And alas that we should have to say it, where vice also erects its head and stalks abroad with an unblushing front, and a fierce hardihood, lamentable to behold. We cannot, to-night, tread its far-famed halls of learning, we may not thread our way through the busy, seething multitudes of its old traditionary streets; but there is one chamber, from whose high windows a solitary light streams out into the murky air, into which we must pass.

It is a plain room, not large, and rich in nothing but books; books which tell the prevalent pursuits, tastes, and studies of its owner, filling the shelves of the little bookcase, covering the table, and piled in heaps on floor and chairs: massive old folios, ponderous quartos, and thick, dumpy little volumes, of the seventeenth century, in faded vellum, seem most to prevail, but there are others with the fresh glitter of modern times without, and perhaps with the false polish of modern philosophies within. With each of its two occupants we have yet to make acquaintance; one is a tall, handsome man, already beyond the freshness of his youth, well-dressed and gentleman-like, but having a disagreeable expression on his finely formed features, and a glittering look in his eye—a look at once exulting and malicious, such as you could fancy of a demon assured of his prey. The other, with whom he is engaged in earnest conversation, is at least ten years his junior; young, sensitive, enthusiastic, he appears to be, with an ample forehead and a brilliant eye, as different as possible in its expression from the shining orb of the other. There is no malice to be seen here, no sneer on those lips, no deceit in that face, open, manly, eloquent and sincere. Famed in his bygone career, he is covered with academic honours, is full of vigour, of promise, of hopefulness, with eloquence on his lips, and logic in his brain, and his mind cultured thoroughly, the favoured of his teachers, the beloved of his companions, the brother of our gentle Christian, our acquaintance of last year in his letter to Christian—Halbert Melville.

But what is this we see to-night! How changed does he seem, then so beautiful, so gallant; there is a fire in his eyes, a wild fire that used not to be there, and the veins are swollen on his forehead, and stand out like whipcord. His face is like the sea, beneath the sudden squall that heralds the coming hurricane, now wild and tossed in its stormy agitation, now lulled into a desperate and deceitful calmness. His lips are severed one moment with a laugh of reckless mirth, and the next, are firmly compressed as if in mortal agony, and he casts a look around as if inquiring who dared to laugh. His arm rests on the table, and his finger is inserted between the pages of a book— one of the glittering ones we can see, resplendent in green and gold—to which he often refers, as the conversation becomes more and more animated; again and again he searches its pages, and after each reference he reiterates that terrible laugh, so wild, so desperate, so mad, while his companion's glittering serpent eye, and sneering lip, send it back again in triumph. What, and why is this?

Look at the book, which Halbert's trembling hand holds open. Look at this little pile laid by themselves in one corner of the room, the gift every one of them of the friend who sits sneering beside him, the Apostle of so-called spiritualism, but in reality, rank materialism, and infidelity, and you will see good cause for the internal struggle, which chases the boiling blood through his youthful veins, and moistens his lofty brow with drops of anguish. The tempter has wrought long and warily; Halbert's mind has been besieged in regular form; mines have been sprung, batteries silenced, bastions destroyed—at least, to Halbert's apprehension, rendered no longer tenable; point by point has he surrendered, stone by stone the walls of the citadel have been undermined, and the overthrowal is complete. Halbert Melville is an unbeliever, an infidel, for the time. Alas! that fair and beauteous structure, one short twelvemonth since so grand, so imposing, so seeming strong and impregnable, lies now a heap of ruins. No worse sight did ever captured fortress offer, after shot and shell, mine and counter-mine, storm and rapine had done their worst, than this, that that noble enthusiastic mind should become so shattered and confused and ruinous.

There is a pause in the conversation. Halbert has shut his book, and is bending over it in silence. Oh, that some ray of light may penetrate his soul, transfix these subtle sophisms, and win him back to truth and right again; for what has he instead of truth and right? only dead negations and privations; a series of Noes—no God, no Saviour, no Devil even, though they are his children; no immortality, no hereafter—a perfect wilderness of Noes. But his tempter sees the danger.

"Come, Melville," he says rising, "you have been studying too long to-day; come man, you are not a boy to become melancholy, because you have found out at last, what I could have told you long ago, that these nonsensical dreams and figments, that puzzled you a month or two since, are but bubbles and absurdities after all—marvellously coherent we must confess in some things, and very poetical and pretty in others—but so very irrational that they most surely are far beneath the consideration of men in these days of progress and enlightenment. Come, you must go with me to-night, I have some friends to sup with me, to whom I would like to introduce you. See, here is your hat; put away Gregg, and Newman, just now, the Nemesis can stand till another time—by-the-by, what a struggle that fellow must have had, before he got to light. Come away."

Poor Halbert yielded unresistingly, rose mechanically, put away the books so often opened, and as if in a dream, his mind wandering and unsettled so that he hardly knew what he was about, he listened to his companion's persuasions, placed his arm within his "friend" Forsyth's, and suffered himself to be led away, the prey in the hands of the fowler, the tempted by the tempter. Poor fallen, forsaken Halbert Melville!

The quiet moments of the winter evening steal along, the charmed hour of midnight has passed over the hoary city, slumbering among its mountains. Through the thick frosty air of that terrible night no moonbeam has poured its stream of blessed light; no solitary star stood out on the clouded firmament to tell of hope which faileth never, and life that endures for evermore, far and long beyond this narrow circuit of joys and sorrows. Dark, as was one soul beneath its gloomy covering, lowered the wide wild sky above, and blinding frost mist, and squalls laden with sleet, which fell on the face like pointed needles, had driven every passenger who had a home to go to, or could find a shelter, or a refuge, from the desolate and quiet streets. In entries, and the mouths of closes, and at the foot of common stairs, little heaps of miserable unfortunates were to be seen huddled together, seeking warmth from numbers, and ease of mind from companionship, even in their vice and wretchedness. Hour after hour has gone steadily, slowly on, and still that chamber is empty, still it lacks its nightly tenant, and the faint gleam of the fire smouldering, shining fitfully, now on the little pile of poison, now on the goodly heaps of what men call dry books and rubbish, but which a year ago Halbert considered as the very triumphs of sanctified genius. Hither and thither goes the dull gleam, but still he comes not.

But hark, there is a step upon the stair, a hurried, feverish, uncertain step, and Halbert Melville rushes into his deserted room, wan, haggard, weary, with despair stamped upon his usually firm, but now quivering lip, and anguish, anguish of the most terrible kind, in his burning eye. He has been doubting, fearing, questioning, falling away from his pure faith—falling away from his devout worship, losing himself and his uprightness of thought, because questioning the soundness of his ancient principles and laying them aside one by one, like effete and worthless things. He has been led forward to doubt by the most specious sophistry—not the rigid unflinching inquiry of a truth-seeker, whose whole mind is directed to use every aid that learning, philosophy, history, and experience can furnish, to find, or to establish what is true and of good repute, but the captious search for seeming flaws and incongruities, the desire to find some link so weak that the whole chain might be broken and cast off. In such spirit has Halbert Melville been led to question, to doubt, to mock, at length, and to laugh, at what before was the very source of his strength and vigour, and the cause of his academical success. And he has fallen—but to-night—to-night he has gone with open eyes into the haunts of undisguised wickedness—to-night he has seen and borne fellowship with men unprincipled, not alone sinning against God, whose existence they have taught Halbert to deny, whose laws they have encouraged him, by their practice and example, to despise, contemn, and set aside, but also against their neighbours in the world and in society. To-night, while his young heart was beating with generous impulses,—while he still loathed the very idea of impurity and iniquity, he has seen the friends of his "friend," he has seen his favoured companion and immaculate guide himself, whose professions of purity and uprightness have often charmed him, who scorned God's laws, because there was that innate dignity in man that needed not an extraneous monitor, whose lofty, pure nature has been to Halbert that long twelvemonth something to reverence and admire; him has he seen entering with manifest delight into all the vile foulness of unrestrained and unconcealed sin, into all the unhallowed orgies of that midnight meeting and debauch. Unhappy Halbert! The veil has been torn from his eyes, he sees the deep, black fathomless abyss into which he has been plunged, the hateful character of those who have dragged him over its perilous brink, who have tempted him to wallow in the mire of its pollutions and to content himself with its flowing wine, its hollow heartless laughter, its dire and loathsome pleasures.

The threatenings of the Scriptures, so long forgotten and neglected, ring now in his terrified ears, like peals of thunder, so loud and stern their dread denunciations. His conscience adopts so fearfully that awful expression,

"The fool hath said in his heart there is no God," that the secret tones of mercy, whispering ever of grace and pardon, are all unheard and unheeded, and he was in great fear, for the Lord is in the generation of the righteous. He leans his burning brow upon the table, but starts back as if stung by an adder, for he has touched one of those fatal books, whose deadly contents, so cunningly used by his crafty tempter, overthrew and made shipwreck of his lingering faith, and has become now a very Nemesis to him. With a shudder of abhorrence and almost fear, he seizes the volume and casts it from him as an unclean thing, and then starts up and paces the room with wild and unsteady steps for a time, then throws himself down again and groans in agony. See! he is trying with his white and quivering lips to articulate the name of that great Being whom he has denied and dishonoured, but the accents die on his faltering tongue. He cannot pray, he fancies that he is guilty of that sin unpardonable of which he has often read and thought with horror. Is he then lost? Is there no hope for this struggling and already sore-tired spirit? Is there no succour in Heaven? The gloom of night gathering thicker and closer round about him, the dying sparkle of the fire, the last faint fitful gleam of the expiring candle leaping from its socket, and as it seems to him soaring away to heaven, cannot answer. Surely there will yet be a morrow.

CHAPTER II.

Alone walkyng. In thought plainyng,
And sore sighying. All desolate
My remembrying Of my livying.
My death wishying Bothe erly and late.

Infortunate, Is so my fate
That wote ye what, Out of mesure
My life I hate; Thus desperate
In such pore estate, Doe I endure.—CHAUCER.

A few weeks have passed away since that terrible night, and we are again in Christian Melville's quiet home. It is on the eve of the new year, but how different is the appearance of those assembled within this still cheerful room from the mirth and happiness which made their faces shine one short twelvemonth since. Our Christian is here, sitting with her head bent down, and her hands clasped together with convulsive firmness. *Here* is little Mary drooping by her side like a stricken flower, while the only other person in the apartment sits sulkily beside them with a discontented, ill-humoured look upon her pretty features, which contrasts strangely, and not at all agreeably, with the pale and anxious faces of her companions—her sisters—for this unhappy looking, discontented woman is James Melville's wife. Strange and terrifying news of Halbert have reached them, "that he has fallen into errors most fatal and hazardous to his future prospects, and all unlike as of his proposed vocation so of his former character, that he had become acquainted and been seen publicly with most unfit and dangerous companions," writes a kind and prudent Professor, who has from the first seen and appreciated the opening promise of Halbert's mind. Two or three days ago James, his brother, has set off to see if these things be true or no, and to bring, if possible and if needful, the wandering erring spirit—we cannot call him prodigal yet—home. The spirit of Christian, the guardian sister, had sunk within her at these terrible tidings; was she not to blame—had she done her part as she ought to have done—had she not been careless—is she guiltless of this sad catastrophe? She remembered Halbert's letter of the past new year—she remembered how studiously he had kept from home all this weary year—she remembered how, save for one hurried visit, he had stayed at a distance from them all, pleading engagements with his friend, that friend that had now proved so deadly a foe. A thousand things, unheeded at the time, sprung up in Christian's memory in lines of fire. The friend of Halbert, free-thinking at the first, what was he? the unwonted restraint of the young brother's correspondence, the studied omission of all reference to sacred things, or to his own prospective avocations in his letters, which in former times used to be the chief subjects of his glowing and hopeful anticipations, the bitterness of tone which had crept into his once playful irony, all these which had only caused a momentary uneasiness, because of her dependence on Halbert's steadfast settled principles, flashed back with almost intolerable distinctness now. Alas! for Christian's recollections—"I am to blame; yes, I ought to have warned him, even gone to him," she thinks; "was he not left me as a precious treasure, to be guarded, to be warned, to be shielded from ill? Oh! that he was home once more." Alas! for Christian's recollections, we say again; the iron fingers of Time measure out the moments of that last lingering hour; again light hearts wait breathless for its pealing signal, as they did of old, but these silent watchers here have no ear for any sounds within their own sorrowful dwelling, though there is not a passing footstep on the street without that does not ring upon their anxious ears in echoing agony; there is not a sound of distant wheels bearing, mayhap, some reveller to and fro, which does not bring an alternate throb and chill to their painful beating hearts. This stillness is past all bearing, it is painfully unendurable, and Christian springs to the door and gazes out upon the cold and cheerless street, and as she does so a thoughtless passenger wishes her a "happy new year." Alas! to speak of happiness, a happy new year to her in such a moment as this!

Mrs. James Melville is astonished at all this grief; she cannot understand nor fathom it. Suppose Halbert *has* been foolish, and behaved ill, what then? Why should her husband have gone off so suddenly, and her sister-in-law be in such a state? She was sure she could not comprehend it, and would have been very foolish to have done such foolish things for all the brothers in the universe. Young men will be young men, and they should be left to come to themselves, instead of all this to-do being made about them; it was preposterous and absurd, and put her in a very ridiculous position; and so Mrs. James pouted and sulked and played with her chains and her rings, stopping now and then in her agreeable relaxation to cast a glance of contemptuous scorn at restless, excited, anxious Christian, and drooping, fragile Mary. A nice way this to bring in the new year, the first anniversary of her married life, the first return of the day of her wedding; a nice state James would be in for her party of to-morrow evening; and Mrs. James, by way of venting her ill-humour, shoved away with her slippered foot, a little dog which was sleeping before the cheerful fire. How Christian starts as it cries and creeps to her feet: it is Halbert's dog, and as her eye falls on it, its youthful owner seems to stand before her, so young, so frank, so innocent! now gay as a child, making the walls echo with his overflowing mirth; now grave and serious, like the dead mother whose latest breath had committed him as a precious jewel to her, and bidden her watch over him and guard him with her life. Oh, had she neglected her charge! Was this fault, this apparent wreck *hers*?

The passing footsteps grew less and less frequent; what can detain them? Old Mr. Melville and his son Robert have gone to meet James and—Halbert—if Halbert be only with him, and Christian trembles as she repeats that pregnant *if*. Her heart will break if they come not soon: she cannot bear this burden of anxiety much longer. Hush! there are footsteps, and they pause at the door. Sick at heart, Christian rushes to it again with little Mary by her side; there at the threshold are her father, James, Robert; she counts them painfully, one by one; but where is Halbert? where is her boy? The long-cherished expectation is at once put to flight; the artificial strength of excitement has gone, and Christian would have fallen to the ground, but for James's supporting arm.

"Christian," he whispered, as he led her back to her seat in the parlour again, "I know you can command yourself, and you must try to do so now, for you will need all your strength to-night."

James's voice was hoarse, and his eyes bloodshot. Where is—what has become of Halbert? The story is soon told. When James reached Edinburgh, he had gone straight to Halbert's lodging, and found when he arrived at it, that his brother had disappeared, gone away, whither the people knew not; his fellow-students and professors were equally ignorant; and all that he could clearly ascertain was, that the reports they had been grieved so much with were too true; that one night some weeks before the day that James went to the lodgings, Halbert had gone out, been seen in several places of the worst character, with men known as profligates, and abandoned, and had come home very late. That since then he had been like a man in despair—mad—his simple landlady said; and she pointed to the books he had left, crowding the shelves and littering the floor of her little room; that two nights before James had arrived—having been shut up all the day—he had gone suddenly out, telling her to send a parcel lying on his table as directed, the next morning. On his mantel-piece was a letter, apparently forgotten, for Christian. "Here it is," said James in conclusion, handing it to her, "would that it could comfort you!"

Christian broke the seal with eager, trembling fingers; perhaps, after all, there might be some comfort here:

"Christian,

"Do not hate me! do not forsake me!" (thus did it begin; and it seemed as if the paper was blistered with tears, so that the words were almost illegible; and thus went on the trembling words of poor Halbert's almost incoherent letter). "I am still your brother; but they will tell you how I have fallen; they will tell you of my guilt—but none—none can tell, can comprehend my misery. I dare not come near you. I dare not return home to pollute the air you breathe with my presence. I feel myself a Cain or a Judas, branded and marked, that all men may shrink from me as from a pestilence; and I must rush out from their sight afar, and from their contact. It is enough that I feel the eye of God upon me—of that God whom I have denied and contemned, whose throne I strove to overturn with my single arm, feeble and frail as it is—continually upon me, on my secret heart burning in on the quivering spirit, my sentence of hopeless, helpless condemnation! They will tell you that I am mad. Oh, that I were, and had been so for these last months, that now I might lose the sense of my sin and of the hopeless despair which haunts me night and day! Christian, I am no infidel, or as the tempters called it, spiritualist now. I shrink and tremble just the same while alone, and when among the crowd, from that terrible Spirit that pursues and searches me out everywhere—terrible in holiness; inexorable in justice, and I cannot pray, 'Be merciful, O thou holy and eternal One.'

"Christian, do you remember that fearful word of Scripture, 'It is impossible to renew them again unto repentance, seeing they crucify to themselves the Son of God afresh, and put him to an open shame?' *I* have entered into the unspeakable bitterness of its doom; it rings in my ears without intermission; 'it is impossible to be renewed again.' But you can pray, Christian; *you* have not cast all hope behind you; and if it is not sin to pray for one accursed, pray for me. It may be I shall never see you again; I know not where I go; I know not what I shall do! There is no peace left for me on earth; and no peace, no hope, no refuge beyond it, that I can see.

"Your brother,
"Halbert Melville."

And where is Christian now? She is lying with rigid marble face and closed eyes, insensible to all the care bestowed upon her, in a dead faint. They are chafing her cold hands and bathing her temples, and using all the readiest means at hand for her recovery. Is Christian gone?—can this letter have killed her?—has she passed away under the pressure of this last great calamity. No: God has happier days in store for his patient servant yet; and by-and-by she is raised from her deathlike faint, and sits up once more; but it seems as if despair had claimed a second prey, so pitiful and mournful is that face, and its expression so changed, that they are all afraid; and little Mary clasps her hand in an agony, and lifts up her tear-stained face to her sister, and whispers—

"Christian! Christian!" in broken, tearful accents.

"We will make every inquiry possible to be made," said James, soothingly; "we may yet bring him back, Christian."

"I don't know what this frenzy means!" says Mr. Melville. "Depend upon it Halbert will come back, and he'll soon see the folly of this outburst of feeling;

and you see, Christian, he says he's no infidel or atheist now, so you need not be so put out of the way by his letter."

Mary says nothing more but "Christian! Christian!" and her arm glides round her sister, and her graceful head rests on Christian's bosom. It is enough: she may not—must not sink down in despair; she has duties to all those around her; she must not give way, but be up and doing.

And there are words of better comfort spoken in her ear to-night ere sleep comes near her; the hand that rocked her cradle in infancy, that tended her so carefully in childhood, draws the curtain gently round her.

"Dinna misdoubt, or lose hope, Miss Christian," sobs old Ailie, her own tears falling thick and fast the while she speaks; "the bairn of sae mony supplications will never be a castaway; he may gang astray for a while, he may be misled, puir lad, or left to himself and fall, and have a heavy weird to dree or a' be done, but he'll no be a lost ane. No, Miss Christian, no, dinna think sae, and distress yoursel' as you're doing—take my word, ye'll baith hear and see guid o' Mr. Halbert yet."

Oh, holy and sublime philosophy, what sure consolation flows in your simple words!

So closes that dawn of the new year on this sorrowing household. Alas, how strange the contrast! A year ago, all, masters and servants, with fervour and enthusiasm, and with heartfelt prayers, wished a "Good, a happy New Year to Halbert" far away; but there is none of that now, Halbert's first year has been a year of trial, mental struggle, and failure so far, and though the same deep love—or even deeper, for these loving hearts cling even more closely to him now, in his time of distress and despair—animates them still, they dare not wish each other, far less openly propose for him, the "happy new year" so usual. Poor household, it may be rich in world's gear, and world's comforts, but the chaplet has lost a rose, and he, so precious to them all, is lost to their ken, vanished from their sight, as it were, and all the remembrance of him that remains is that of a "broken man."

But where is Halbert? Away, in a struggling ship, tossing on the stormy bosom of the wide Atlantic, alone upon the storm-swept deck, whence everything, not fastened with wood and iron, has been driven by these wintry seas; boats, bulwarks, deck load and lumber, are all gone into the raging deep, and yet he stands on the deck, drenched by every sea, watching the giant billows, before which all but he are trembling, uncovered, while the lightning gleams athwart the seething waters, and the thunder peals out in incessant volleys overhead; unsheltered, while the big raindrops pour down in torrents from the heavy cloud-laden sky. There is no rest for him; in vain does he stretch himself in his uneasy cot; in vain forces the hot eyelid to close upon the tearless eye; since he wrote Christian, all weeping and tears have been denied him. Sleep, which comes in healing quietness to all his shipmates, does not visit him; or, if for a moment wrapped in restless slumbers, dreams of fearful import rise up before him, far surpassing in their dread imagery the gloomiest and most horrible conceptions of his waking thoughts or fancy, too horrible to bear; and the wretched dreamer starts out into the dreary air, thinking himself a veritable Jonah, to whom this tempest and these stormy seas are sent as plagues, and he stands a fit spectator of that external elemental warfare, which is but a type and emblem, fierce though it be, of the raging war within.

See, how he stands, invulnerable in his despair, the strong masts quivering like wands in the furious tempest, the yards naked, and not a rag of sail that would stand before it for an instant; the decks swept by the sea at every moment, and nothing looked for now, by the staunchest seaman on board, but utter and speedy destruction. "The ship cannot stand this much longer," whispers the captain to his chief mate; "she'll founder in an hour, or become water-logged, which would be as bad, or worse, at this season and in this latitude. Stand by for whatever may happen." And yet, all this time, there is not an eye in that strained and struggling ship but Halbert's, that does not shrink from looking upon the boiling sea; there is not a heart but his, however hardened or obdurate it be, which does not breathe some inward prayer, though it be but some half-forgotten infant's rhyme. But Halbert Melville stands alone, uncompanioned, and uncomplaining in his secret grief; no blessed tear of sorrow hangs on the dark lash of his fevered eye; no syllable of supplication severs his parched lips; the liberal heavens, which drop grace upon all, are shut, in his agonised belief, to him alone. He cannot weep; he dare not pray.

EPOCH III.

There's joy and mourning wondrously entwined
In all that's mortal: sometimes the same breeze
That bringeth rest into one weary mind
Heralds another's sorer agonies;
Sometimes the hour that sees one battle end
Beholds as sad a time of strife begin;
And sometimes, hearts rejoicing as they win
Themselves the victory, tremble for a friend.
Ah me! how vain to think that mortal ken
Can ever, with love-cleared vision, judge aright.
Doth danger dwell alone 'mong stranger men,
Or safety aye 'neath home's protecting light?
Shield us, our Father! in our every lot
Thou blendest joy and grief that we forget thee not.

CHAPTER I.

Then followed that beautiful season,
Called by the pious Acadian peasants the summer of All Saints!
Filled was the air with a dreamy and magical light; and the landscape
Lay as if new created in all the freshness of childhood.
Peace seemed to reign upon earth, and the restless heart of the ocean
Was for a moment consoled.—LONGFELLOW'S *Evangeline*.

TWO years have worn on their slow course, two tedious, weary years, and the first days of December have again arrived. We are now under a sunnier sky than that of England, and on the outskirts of an old, wide-spreading, perhaps, primeval forest, full of giant pines and hemlocks, and the monarch oak, beside which the axe of the back-woodsman has never yet been lifted. It is morning, and the sun gleams on the brilliant, dewy leaves of trees, in detached and scattered groups, each clad like the beloved of Jacob in his coat of many colours. The Indian summer, pleasant and evanescent, is on the wane, and there is a soft murmur of falling leaves, as the morning breeze steals through the rustling foliage, and save for that, and the usual sounds of the forest—the diapason of that natural organ—all is still, and hushed, and silent. We are on the eve of winter, we witness the russet leaves falling before every breath of wind, but yet the grass is as green as ever, and wild flowers and creepers, luxuriant among the tangled under-brush, festoon the branches with their hanging blossoms. Here is one leafy arcade, where sunshine and shadow dance in tremulous alternation on the soft velvety turf beneath; and hark! the silence is broken; there are the sounds of footsteps on the green sward, the crackling of dried twigs which have fallen, and the sounds of some approaching creature. The charm is broken, into this natural temple some one has entered; who can it be, and for what end does he come?

Down this arcade comes the intruder, deeper and deeper into the forest; he seems to have no settled purpose here, but wanders below the drooping branches in meditative silence, communing with his heart, and inhaling as it seems the melancholy tenderness which floats in the shadowy air—melancholy because anticipating the departure of those bright lingerers in summer's lengthened train; and tender, because remembering how Nature, the universal mother, gathers in beneath her wintry mantle those children of her care, and nourishes them in her genial bosom till spring robes her anew with their verdure and their flowers. He seems no stranger to these gentle sympathies, this solitary wayfarer, but looks upon the gay foliage and clinging flowers as if they were ancient friends. He is young, but there is a shadow on his face which tells of mental suffering and grief, though it seems of grief whose agony and bitterness has past away. His face is thin, worn, and thoughtful, there are deep furrows on his cheek and brow, the traces of some great and long-enduring struggle; his eyes are cast down, and his lips move from time to time, as though they were repeating words of comfort, with which he was striving to strengthen himself, and ever and anon he anxiously raises his earnest eyes to heaven, as if he sought for light to his soul and assurance there; and then again his head is bent down towards the greensward as if in sudden humility, and a sigh of conscious guilt or unworthiness breaks from his labouring breast, and he writhes as if he felt a sudden agonising pang. It is evident that this lonely man seeks for something which he has not, of the lack of which he is fully conscious, and which he desires with all the intensity of a soul's most ardent and earnest longing to obtain; wealth it cannot be, nor fame, nor honour, for this wild wilderness, this place so solitary and far from the abodes of men, is not where these are either sought or found. On the trunk of a giant pine which lies across the green arcade, a trophy of the last winter's storms, he seats himself; the gentle gale breathes through the wood in long low sighings, which come to the ear like a prolonged moan; the leaves fall softly with a pleasant plaintive cadence to their mossy grave; the sun looks down from the heavens, veiling his glory with a cloud, as though he feared to gaze too keenly on a scene so fair and solemn; the heart of the lonely meditative man is fairly melted within him; the object he has been searching for, which he has so longed to possess, which has shone upon him hitherto so distant, so far off, beyond the reach of his extended hand, and never been seen save in such transient glimpses of his straining eyes that again and again, and yet again, his doubts and fears have returned in almost their original force, and the despair, which almost engulfed him in the old sad time, seems near at hand to enshroud him once again, is suddenly brought to nearest neighbourhood. A holy presence fills that quiet air; a voice of love, and grace, and mercy steals into that long bereaved and mourning heart; he throws himself down on the dewy grass, and its blades bend beneath heavier and warmer drops than the soft tears of morn and even. Listen! for his voice breaks through the stillness with a tone of unspeakable joy, thrilling in its accents, and its words are "all things;" hark how the wind echoes them among the trees, as though so worthy of diffusion, so full of hopeful confidence, that even it loved to linger on and prolong the sound. "All things are possible—with God." His trembling form is bent in the hallowed stillness of unuttered prayer; his frame quivers with an emotion for years unfelt. Oh! how different from all his past shakings and tremblings, how different from all that has gone before is this! But who dare lift the veil which covers the deep humility of that supplicating spirit, or break in upon the holy confidence with which it approaches, in this its first communion, its God and Father. It is enough that there is joy in heaven, this blessed morning, over the returned prodigal, the lost and wandering child, "he that was dead is alive again, he that was lost is found," and Halbert Melville at length is at rest.

Long and fearfully has he struggled since that fearful night in hoary Edinburgh; been tossed in Atlantic storms, seen the wonders of the Lord on the great deep, in the thunder, and the lightning, and the tempest, and experienced His goodness in being brought to land in safety once again. For years since then, on every wall, his tearless eyes have seen, as though written by an unseen hand, those terrible words, "It is impossible," and a voice heard by no mortal but himself, has rung again and again in sad reiteration into his despairing ears, "It is impossible," like an "anathema maranatha," ever binding and irreversible. But to-day the whole has changed, the cloud has been dissipated and the sun shines forth once more; another voice sweeter than that harp of sweetest sound has brought to him joy for mourning, and blotted out from his mental horizon his fancied doom, with that one word of gracious omnipotence, "All things are possible with God." It has told him of the might that can save to the uttermost, of the grace that casts away no contrite heart, and of the love to sinners which passeth all knowledge; and in the day of recovered hope, and in faith which has already the highest seal, the spirit's testimony ennobling its meek humility, Halbert Melville arises from beneath these witness trees, from that altar in a cathedral of Nature's own fashioning for its Maker's worship, more grand and noble than the highest conception of man could conceive or his highest art embellish, with a change wrought upon his enfranchised spirit, which makes him truly blessed. In his despair and hopelessness he had pronounced this "impossible," and he stands now rejoicing in the glorious words of one of old, "Return unto thy rest, oh, my soul! for the Lord hath dealt bountifully with thee." The summer was nearly past, the winter had nearly come, but Halbert Melville was saved.

But Halbert must go home; alas, he has no home in this wide continent. In all the multitude of breathing mortals here, there is not one whose eye grows brighter or heart warmer at his approach. He is, on the contrary, regarded curiously and with wonder; sometimes indeed with pity, but he is still the stranger, though nearly two years have passed since first he received that name. His home, such as it is, is in a great bustling town, at a distance from this quiet solitude, to which long ago—there are places near it famed in the catalogue of vulgar wonders,—a sudden impulse drew him, a yearning to look on nature's sunny face again, as he had done of old in his days of peace and happiness, or a desire, it might be, to attain even a deeper solitude than he, stranger though he was, could find amid the haunts of men. But now he must return to his distasteful toil, and solitary room. Ah! Halbert, how different from the solitary room in old Edinburgh, the books, congenial studies, and pleasant recreations before the tempter came! but it is with a light step and a contented heart for all that, that Halbert Melville retraces his steps along the lonely way. Now there is hope in the sparkle of his brightened eye, and a glow of his own old home affections at his heart, as he catches the wide sweep of the distant sea, and the white sails swelling already in the pleasant breeze, that will bear them home. Home! what magic in the word! it has regained all its gladdening power, that hallowed syllable, and Halbert is dreaming already of Christian's tearful welcome, and little Mary's joy; when a chill strikes to his heart. Is he sure that the letter of the prodigal, who has brought such agony and grief upon them, will be received so warmly? No, he is not, he doubts and fears still, for all the peace that is in his heart, and Halbert's first resolution is changed; he dare not write; but his fare shall be plain, his lodging mean, his apparel scanty, till he has the means of going home, of seeking pardon with his own lips, of looking on their reconciled faces with his own rejoicing eye; or of bidding them an adieu for evermore.

Halbert has reached the noisy town again, and is threading his way through its busy streets, among as it seems the self-same crowd he traversed on his departure; but how differently he looks on it now; then he noticed none but the poor, the aged, the diseased; and thought in the selfishness of engrossing care, that the burdens which they bore were light in comparison with that which weighed him down. Now he embraces them all in the wide arms of his new-born and sympathetic philanthropy, and is as ready in the fulness of his heart to rejoice with them that do rejoice, as to weep with those that weep. His was a true, an early love, which flies to make its master's presence known to those who are out of the way; who see him not, or seeing understand not; and laden with its own exceeding joy, yearns to share it with all who stand in need of such peace and rest as he himself has found.

But now he has entered his own dwelling, just as the sudden gloom of the American night, unsoftened by gentle twilight, falls thick and dark around. It is a place where many like himself in years, station, and occupations, engaged in the counting-houses of that great commercial city, have their abode. Young men gay and careless, with little thought among them for anything beyond the business or amusement of the passing hour. A knot of such are gathered together in the common sitting-room when Halbert enters; but they scarcely interrupt their conversation to greet him: he has kept apart from all of them, and almost eschewed their society or companionship. The night is cold, it has grown chilly with the lengthening shadows, and a glowing fire of logs burns brightly and cheerfully upon the hearth, and Halbert, wearied and cold, seats himself beside it. The conversation goes on, it flags not because the stranger is an auditor; one young man there is in this company, a merry scoffer, whose witty sallies are received with bursts of laughter, the rather because just now, and indeed usually, they are directed against Scripture and holy things. There is another who inveighs against the fanaticism and bigotry of some portion of the Church, which is, according to his foolish notion, righteous over much, and therefore, in his clear and conclusive logic, the Church universal is only a piece of humbug; and there is a third whom Halbert has long marked, a cold argumentative heartless sceptic, who, emboldened by the profane mirth of the other young men around him, has begun to broach his infidel opinions, and for them finds a favourable auditory. Look at Halbert's face now, how it beams in the fire-light, as he hears the cold-blooded insinuations, and words of blasphemy, the dead negations, the poison of his own heedless youth, from which he has suffered so sorely, again propounded in the identical guise and semblance which bewitched himself of old. See him! how his dark eyes sparkle with righteous fire; how his bent form grows erect and stately, and his features expand in unconscious nobility, as though there was inspiration within his heart, because of which he must interfere, must speak to these youths, should he perish.

The solitary man bends over the cheerful blaze no longer. See him among these wondering youths, with the light of earnest truth beaming from every noble line of his prophet face. Listen to his solemn tone, his words of weighty import. Hear what he says to them, amazed and confounded that the stranger has at last found a voice. What does he say? he tells the story of his own grievous shipwreck; he tells them how he was tempted and how he fell; tells them of all the wiles and stratagems by which he was overcome, and how he found out only at the very last, how hollow, false, and vain they were; bids them remember the miserable man bowed down by secret sorrow, that they have all along known him, and his voice trembles with solemn earnestness, as he warns them as they love their lives—as they love the gladness which God has given them, the heritage of their youth—to refuse and reject the insinuations of the tempter, and to oppose themselves to the serpent-cunning of the blasphemer, refusing even to listen to his specious arguments and hollow one-sided logic, if they wish it to be well with them. The air of the room has grown suddenly too hot for the discomfited sceptic, the scoffer has forgotten his gibe, the grumbler his grievance, and their companions their responsive laughter. Halbert's words of sad and stern experience, spoken in solemn warning, sink into their hearts with much effect, at least for the time. Perhaps the impression will not last, but at this moment, these thoughtless youths are startled into seriousness, and whatever the effect may be ultimately, the recollection of that thrilling appeal will linger, and that for long, in their memories.

Sweet slumber and pleasant dreams has Halbert Melville this night. He lies in that fair chamber, whose windows open to the rising sun, where rested after his great fight of afflictions that happy dreamer of old, where peace is, and no visions of terror can enter, and Halbert Melville, whatever his future fate may be, whether calm or tempest, fair or foul weather, has like the pilgrim found rest.

CHAPTER II.

Maiden! with the meek brown eyes,
In whose orb a shadow lies,
Like the dusk in evening skies!
*   *   *   *   *
O, thou child of many prayers!
Life hath quicksands—Life hath snares!
Care and age comes unawares!—LONGFELLOW.

IT is well that there are swifter ways of mental travel, than even the very quickest means of transit for the heavier material part, or we should be too late, even though we crossed the Atlantic in the speediest steamer of these modern days, and with the fairest winds and weather, for Mrs. James Melville's new year's party. Mrs. James looks none the worse for these two years that have glided away since we saw her last; she is dressed in all her holiday smiles to-night, though, as you pass up the lighted staircase to her drawing-room, you can hear a shrill tone of complaint coming from some far-off nursery, which shows that James's pretty house has got another tenant; and, truly, his paternal honours sit well on our old friend. The street without is illuminated by the lights which gleam through the bright windows, and are alive with the mirth and music that is going on within. There is a large company assembled; and, amid the crowded faces, all so individual and dissimilar, beaming on each other, here is one we should know—pale, subdued, and holy, like the Mary of some old master. It seems out of place, that grave, sweet countenance in this full room, and among this gay youthful company. It is our old friend Christian, hardly, if at all, changed since last we saw her, save for her deepened, yet still not melancholy sadness; it is said that her smiles, since that terrible time of Halbert's disappearance, have been more sad than other people's tears, but she does smile sweetly and cheerfully still; there is too little of the gall of humanity about her, too little selfishness in her gentle spirit to permit the cloud, which hovers over her own mind, to darken with its spectre presence the enjoyment of others. Christian likes—as may be well believed—the quietness of her own fireside better than any other place; but James would have been grieved had she stayed away, and therefore is she here amid this crowd to-night. But there is a graceful figure near her that we shall not recognise so easily, though coming from a contemplation of that thin, worn face, inspired as we saw it last in yonder American city, and looking as we do on Christian there before us, we see that the features of her brilliant countenance are as like as brothers and sisters may be—like, and yet unlike, for the pressure of that great sorrow has fallen lightly on little Mary's buoyant spirit. She is still "little Mary," though her head is higher now than Christian's, who calls her so. Those two years have added no less to her inner growth than to her stature, and Mary Melville, with all the mirth and joyousness of her earlier girlhood, has the cultivated mind of a woman now. There are many bright young faces shining in this gay room, but there is not one like little Mary's; not one eye in this assembly can boast such a sunny glance as hers, graver than her peers when it is called to look on serious things, and beaming then with a youthful wisdom, which tells of holy thoughts and pure intents within, and anon illumined with such a flash of genuine mirthfulness and innocent gaiety, so fresh and unconscious in its happy light, as would startle the sternest countenance into an answering smile. She is much loved, our sprightly Mary, and is the very sun and light of the circle she moves in; and friends who have known her from her childhood, tell one another how like she is to Halbert, and shake their heads, and are thankful that she can never be exposed to similar temptations. Do they think that Mary, like her brother, would have fallen, that she must succumb too, before the adversary's power, if tried as hardly? Ah, it is not well that the innocent lamb, so tender, so guileless and gentle, should be exposed to the power of the wolf, and who can tell but that there may be deadly danger lurking about her even now.

Christian's smile grows brighter as it falls on Mary, "little Mary's" sparkling face, and her voice is happier and more musical in its modulation as she answers her affectionate inquiries. They speak truly who say that Christian has no thought of herself: at this hour Christian would fain be on her knees in her solitary room, pleading for her lost brother; not lost, deaf Christian, say not lost—is there not a lingering tone of sweet assurance in thy mournful heart, which, if thou would'st but hear it, speaks to thee out of the unknown secret stillness and says, Not lost, not lost, dear Christian, though thou yet knowest not how the faithful One has answered thy weeping prayers.

But, hush! little Mary is singing; a simple plaintive melody, as natural in its pleasant notes, as the dropping of the withered leaves around her absent brother, in yon far American forest. There is a charm in these old songs which far surpasses more artistic music, for scarce is there a single ear on which they fall that has not many remembrances and associations awakened, or recalled, it may be joyful, it may be sorrowful, connected with their simple measure and well-known words, and in such, and in no other, does Mary Melville delight. There is one sitting by Mary's side who seems to comprehend what few of the listeners do, or care to do, the singer's delicate and sweet expression of the feeling of her well-chosen song. He has never seen her before to-night, but he seems to have made wonderfully good use of the short time he has spent beside her; and Mary has already discovered that the gentleman-like stranger, who devoted himself to her all through the evening, is a remarkably well-informed, agreeable man, and quite superior to the frivolous youths who generally buzz about in Elizabeth's drawing-room, and form the majority of her guests. He has brilliant conversational powers, this stranger, and the still more remarkable art of drawing out the latent faculty in others, and Mary is half-ashamed, as she sees herself led on to display her hoards of hidden knowledge, adorned with her own clear perceptions of the true and beautiful, which, unknown to herself, she has acquired. It is a strange, an unusual thing with Mary to meet with any mind, save Christian's, which can at all appreciate her own, and she is rejoicing in her new companion's congenial temperament, and, in a little while, there is a group of listeners collected round them, attracted by something more interesting than the vapid conversations which are going on in this large room. Mr. Forsyth's accomplishments are universally acknowledged, and he shines resplendent to night; and one after another, dazzled by his sparkling wit and still more engaging seriousness, join the circle, of which Mary is still the centre.

"Who would have thought," say we, with Mrs. James, as she gazes wonderingly over the heads of her guests on the animated face of her young sister-in-law,—"who would have thought that Mary knew so much, or could show it so well!"

Is Christian's care asleep to-night; what is she doing that she is not now watching over her precious charge? No, it is not; her eyes, which have strayed for a moment, are now resting fixed on Mary. See! how her cheek flushes at that man's graceful deference. Listen to the laugh that rings from the merry circle at some sally of his polished wit. Mary looks grave and anxious for a moment, for his jest has just touched something which she will not laugh at, and he perceives it, and at once changes his tone, and turns with polished ease the conversation into a new channel. Is it well that Christian should be ignorant of one who is engrossing so much of her sister's attention? No, it is not; and she feels that it is not; so she calls James, and is even now, while Mary's joyousness is returning, anxiously inquiring of her brother who this stranger is. James does not even know his name. A cousin of Elizabeth's brought him to-night, and introduced him as a friend who had been of great service to him; then Elizabeth herself is appealed to; Mrs. James is quite sure that Mr. Forsyth is a very respectable, as well as a very agreeable man; he could never have found his way into her drawing-room had he been other than that; her cousin never would have brought him had he not been quite certain and satisfied on that point. He is very rich, she believes, and very accomplished, she is sure, and, being unmarried, she is extremely pleased to see him paying so much attention to Mary. Christian shudders—why, she does not know; but she feels that this is not well, there is a something in his look—such nonsense! But Christian has always such strange, such peculiar notions, and is so jealous of all that approach Mary.

The gay young people that are around Mary make room for Christian, as she glides in to sit down by her sisters's side. She is very grave now, as always; but some of them have heard her story, and all the nature in their hearts speaks for her in tones of sympathy, and their voices are quieter always when beside her. Over most of them she has some other power besides this of sympathetic feeling; there is hardly one there to whom she has not done some deed of quiet kindness, which would not even bear acknowledgment; thus they all love Christian. She sits down by Mary's side, and her heart grows calmer, and more assured again; for Mary bends over her, and seeks forgiveness for her momentary forgetfulness. Pardon from Christian is easily obtained; yet, gentle as she is, it seems not so easy to win her favour. Mr. Forsyth's fascinating powers, displayed and exerted to the full, are all thrown away. See how coldly she listens to and answers him; nay, how impatient she is of his courteous attentions. What has he done wrong? what can ail Christian?

Mr. James Melville's party has been a very brilliant one; but it is all over now: the street grows suddenly sombre and silent opposite the darkened windows, and Mrs. James is not in the sweetest of moods: the baby, now that all the other music has ceased, is exercising his vigorous lungs for the amusement of the tired household; his weary mamma is aggravated into very ill-humour, and unfortunately can find no better way of relieving herself, nor any better object, than by railing at Christian's folly. Mrs. James is sure, if Mr. Forsyth were to think of Mary Melville, they might all of them be both proud and pleased, for he would be an excellent match for her. She could not think what Christian expected for her—some unheard-of prodigy she fancied, that nobody but herself ever dreamt of—thus did the lady murmur on to the great annoyance of James.

But we must leave Mrs. James and her indignation to themselves, that we may follow the sisters home. They had little conversation on the way. Christian was silent and absorbed in her own thoughts, and Mary wondered, but did not disturb her; for Mary, too, has thoughts unusual, which she cares not to communicate; and soon, again, we are in the old room, no way changed since we saw it first, three years ago; and Mr. Melville—how shall we excuse ourselves for passing him over so lightly and so long—is here unaltered, as much a fixture in his wide, soft chair, as any piece of furniture in the well-filled room; and Robert, we lost him amid the belles of Mrs. James's party! but here he is again, distinct, full grown and manly, and still retaining the blithe look of old. Christian alone has yet a disturbed apprehensive expression on her usually calm and placid face, and she wonders,

"How can James like such parties? it is so different from his wont."

"Yes," says Mary innocently, "I wonder that Elizabeth likes them. If there were just two or three intelligent people like Mr. Forsyth, it would be so much better."

Poor Christian!

The protection of the Almighty has been implored "through the silent watches of the night," and Mr. Melville's household is hushed in sleep—all but Christian; for this quiet hour when all are at rest, is Christian's usual hour of thoughtful relaxation and enjoyment. But she had a clouded brow and an uneasy look when she entered her room to-night—that room of many memories. At length there is no mist of disquietude to be seen upon her peaceful face; no doubt in her loving heart: she has gone to the footstool of the Lord, and borne with her there that child of her tenderness and affection, over whose dawning fate she has trembled, and has committed her into the keeping of the Father of all; and she has poured forth, with weeping earnestness, the longings of her soul for that lost brother, whom even yet she knows not to be within the reach of prayer. Often has she thought that Halbert may be dead, since day after day these years have come and gone, and no tidings from, or of him, have gladdened her heart. Her spirit has been sick with deferred hope, as month after month went by and brought no message. But she is calmer to-night; the load is off her soul; she has entrusted the guardianship of the twain into His hands who doeth all things well, and with whom all things are possible; and wherefore should she fear!

The light in her chamber is extinguished, and the moonbeams are streaming in through the window. A few hours since she watched their silvery radiance stealing, unheeded and unseen, into yon crowded room, drowned in the flood of artificial light which filled it, and then she had thought these rays an emblem of Heaven's Viceroy—conscience—unknown and unnoticed, perchance, by those gay people round about her, but even then marking with silent finger upon its everlasting tablets, the hidden things of that unseen and inner life in long detail, moment, and hour, and day, for each one of them. But now, in the silence of her own room, these beams have another similitude to Christian, as they pour in unconfined, filling the quiet chamber. They tell her of peace, peace full, sweet, and unmeasured,—not the peace of a rejoicing and triumphant spirit,—the sunbeams are liker it,—but of one borne down with trial and sorrow, with a sore fight of affliction, with a fear and anguish in times past, yet now at rest. Oh, happy contradiction! distracted with cares and anxieties, yet calm amid them all, full of the memories of bygone sorrow, of forebodings of sorrows yet to come, but peaceful withal, how blessed the possession!

It falls upon her form, that gentle moonshine, and her features are lit up as with a twilight ray of heaven: it lingers over her treasures as though it loved them for her sake. It streams upon that portrait on the wall, and illuminates its pensive and unchanging face, as with the shadow of a living smile; and Christian's heart grows calm and still within her beating breast, like an infant's, and holy scenes of old come up before her liquid eyes, like ancient pictures, with that steadfast face upon the wall shining upon her in every one; not so constant in its sad expression, but varying with every varying scene, till the gathering tears hang on her cheeks like dewdrops, and she may not look again.

And there is peace in that household this night, peace and sweet serenity, and gentle hopefulness; for a blessing is on its prayer-hallowed roof and humble threshold, and angels stand about its quiet doorway, guarding the children of their King—the King of Kings.

EPOCH IV.

There is no emblem of our lives so fit
As the brief days of April, when we sit
Folding our arms in sorrow, our sad eyes
Dimmed with long weeping; lo! a wondrous ray,
Unhoped-for sunshine bursting from the skies
To chase the shadow of our gloom away.
And lest the dazzling gladness blind us, lo!
An hour of twilight quiet followeth slow,
Moistening our eyelids with its grateful tears,
Strengthening our vision for the radiant beam
That yet shall light these unknown future years,—
Each joy, each grief, in its appointed room,
Ripening the precious fruit for heaven's high harvest home.

CHAPTER I.

Benedict. Pray thee, sweet Mistress Margaret, deserve well at my hands by helping me to the speech of Beatrice.

* * * * *

Sweet Beatrice, wouldst thou come when I called thee?
Much ado about Nothing.

WE are half inclined to lament that the incidents of our story confine us to one short month, nay, oftener to one little day of every passing year, but nevertheless so it is, and we may not murmur. Doubtless could we have sketched the glories of some midsummer morning or autumnal night, or wandered by our heroine's side through the gowan-spotted braes in the verdant springtime, we should have had pleasanter objects to describe, and a pleasanter task in describing them, and our readers a less wearisome one in following us; but seeing that we must, perforce, abide by "the chamber and the dusky hearth," even so, let it be. The hearth of our present sketch is in nowise dusky, however; there is nothing about it that is not bright as the blazing fire itself. If you look from the window you may see that everything without is chained down hard and fast in the iron fetters of the frost, and covered with a mantle of dazzling whiteness. With tenacious grasp the wintry king fixes the less obdurate snow to the heavy housetops, decking them as with hood and mantle; with malicious glee it rivets each drop of spilt water on the slippery pavement, bringing sudden humiliation, downfall and woe, to the heedless passengers; and from the southern eaves where the sun has for some short time exerted a feeble power, hang long icicles in curious spirals, like the curls of youthful beauty. Keen and cold, it revels in the piercing wind, which coming from the bleak north in full gush round the chill street corner, aggravates the wintry red and blue which battle for the mastery in the faces of the shivering passengers, and screams out its chill laughter in the gale, when some sturdy man who has but now chased its little glowing votaries from their icy play is suddenly overthrown himself by one incautious step, and with prostration lower than Eastern does homage to its power, to the great and loudly expressed satisfaction of the urchins aforesaid, who have resumed again their merry game with renewed zeal and vigour.

It is just the kind of morning to make dwellers at home hug themselves on their comfortable superiority over those whom necessity calls abroad, to dare the dangerous passage of these treacherous streets and meet the rough encounters of the biting wind. The room we stand in is the very picture of neatness and comfort; a beautiful infant of two years old is roaming with unsteady step about the bright fireside and over the carpet, a wide world to him, intently making voyages of discovery hither and thither, among the chairs and tables, the continents and islands of his navigation; and beside a pretty work-table, with her delicate fingers employed in still more delicate work, sits Mrs. James Melville, her brow furrowed and curved in deliberative wisdom, giving earnest heed to schemes which are being poured into her attentive ear, and ever and anon responding with oracular gravity. Who is this that seeks and has obtained the infinite benefit of Mrs. James's counsel, and that now with deferential courtesy lays before her the inexpressible advantages he will derive from her advice and assistance, and insinuates the unending gratitude of which he has already given earnest in delicate and well-timed presents, such as delight a lady's heart? He is speaking of a brilliant establishment to be offered to some one whom he seeks to win, and shall win all the more easily through his kind friend Mrs. James's advice and co-operation. He is speaking of wealth which hitherto he laments,—and here the petitioner sighs and looks, or tries to look pathetic,—he has not properly employed, wherewith that as yet nameless third party shall be endowed, and he winds up all with an eulogium upon the extraordinary ability, and undeserved, but not unappreciated kindness of the lady who smiles so graciously at his well-timed compliments. Mrs. James is completely won over, and her full assistance and co-operation pledged, for the pleader is skilled in his craft, and wont to be successful. Who can resist Mr. Forsyth's eloquence and special reasonings? The work of consultation goes on, the toils are laid for Mary, sweet Mary Melville's unwitting feet, and Forsyth, on the strength of his ally's assurances, has already brightened in anticipatory triumph, and if all things be as Mrs. James says they are, and all Forsyth's promises be realised, is not Mary's lot a bright one? Nay, but is this a man to hold in his hands the happiness of Christian's sister?

Mrs. James is determined to signalise herself as a match-maker, and there are a thousand captivating circumstances which conspire to make her eager in the furtherance of Forsyth's suit. She reckons up some of them: First, it will really be an excellent settlement for Mary; where among her father's hum-drum acquaintance could she ever have found one anything at all like so good; secondly, Mrs. Forsyth's wealth and style will bring even her, Mrs. James Melville, into a more brilliant sphere; and above all, there will be the crowning delight of overcoming, or rather being able to set at nought, all Christian's opposition. Mrs. James, self-confident as she is, very bold, and even impertinent as she can be at some times, and strong in the might of superior elegance and beauty, has always been awed in the presence of Christian's quiet dignity, and this had annoyed and galled her greatly. There is something in that grave dignity which she cannot comprehend, and still more aggravating is the fact, that do what she will, she cannot quarrel with her gentle sister-in-law, and that all her innuendoes fall pointless and harmless. Christian will not hear Mrs. James's petulance, be it ever so loud, for with one calm word she shows her its insignificance; she smiles at her sarcasms against old maids, as she might smile at some nick-name of childish sport; nay, sometimes, and it is the nearest approach to mirth which Christian is ever known to make *now*, she will turn round in defence of the maligned sisterhood, and chase with lightfooted raillery, which savours of days of old, the heavy wit of her opponent off the field. Mrs. James never saw Christian ruffled or disturbed by any speech of hers, save on that occasion which introduced Forsyth to Mary, and she was too watchful and too much delighted to let the opportunity of prolonging her annoyance cease; and Mary, a frequent visitor at her brother's house, has since that time, nearly a year now, met her sister-in-law's accomplished acquaintance so often, that people begin to whisper about Forsyth's devotion, and to look forward to a bridal; and when he is spoken of before Mary, they smile and look in her face, and the colour on her soft cheek deepens, and the blood flushes on her forehead, and then when they wonder at his versatile talents, as they often do, for he is intellectually in that society a giant among dwarfs, Mary's downcast eyelids grow wet with pleasant moisture, and her heart thrills with pleasure, so that she, loving Christian as she does, is unconsciously furthering Mrs. James in her plan of annoyance. Our poor Mary!

But we are neglecting the conversation which is still going on between Mrs. James and her visitor. Forsyth is preparing to go, his visit has been already prolonged beyond all usual bounds, yet he lingers still, endeavouring with his persuasive eloquence to bring about one other arrangement.

"You will bring Mary here to meet me, on new year's day morning, my dear madam?" he says softly, and in the most insinuating tone, "will you not?"

"New year's morning," interrupted Mrs. James, "that will never do. You know I have always a party on the new year's night, I shall not be able to give you that morning."

"Well," answered Forsyth, as smoothly and persuasively as he could, "but if you could give us your presence for a few minutes, Mary and I, I hope, will be able to manage the rest ourselves, and you know, my dear Mrs. Melville," he added still more blandly, "I am anxious to come to an understanding with Mary as soon as possible. Come, you must add this to the many kindnesses you have done me already. You will consent, I see."

Mrs. James could not resist. "Well then, on new year's morning be here, and Mary shall meet you," she said, and her gratified friend bows over her extended hand. "You may come, Mr. Forsyth, on new year's morning."

Mr. Forsyth can never sufficiently express his obligation; and having succeeded in all things according to his wish with Mrs. James Melville, he takes his leave at last, and rejoices as he hurries through the streets, so cold and bitter to other passengers, but so bright and cheerful to him in his present mood, that soon now he will be assured of Mary. He has no doubt about it, none at all, and he is certain that all that he wants is just this opportunity which Mrs. James is to secure him, and then Mary Melville will be his own, plighted and pledged his own.

It is but a few days, yet new year's morning is as tardy in approach as if, so big with fate to that young, ingenious, and unfearful spirit, it lingered on its way willing to prolong her state of happy unconsciousness. The elegant Mr. Forsyth yawns through the long weary days; though it is the time of his own appointing he is impatient and restless, and his yawning and irksomeness is redoubled on that dull, cold, cheerless evening before its dawn, and he gets really nervous as the time draws near. Strange that one so practised in the world, whose heart has been so long a very superfluous piece of matter, should have his dead affections so powerfully awakened by the simple grace and girlish beauty of guileless Mary Melville. Strange, indeed, and if he is successful in winning her—as who can doubt he will—what hope is there for our sweet Mary when his sudden vehement liking passes into indifference. Poor Mary's constant heart should be mated only with one as warm and as full of affection and tenderness as itself; but who shall have the choosing of their own future—alas, who! or who, if the choice was given them, would determine aright?—not Mary. But there is a power, the bridegroom in anticipation wots not of, ordering the very words which shall fall from his lips to-morrow, overruling the craftiness of his crafty and subtle spirit, and guarding the innocent simplicity of the prayer-protected girl, defending her from all ill.

CHAPTER II.

York. I'll not be by, the while; My Liege, farewell;
What will ensue hereof, there's none can tell;
But by bad courses may be understood
That these events can never fall out good.
King Richard the Second.

NEW YEAR'S day at last arrived, the time so anxiously waited for by Forsyth; a cold clear winter morning; and Mary, invited specially by her sister-in-law, leaves home to help—to help in some little preparations for the evening, was the reason or plea assigned by Mrs. James to secure Mary on that morning; and even Christian had nothing to object to a request so reasonable, though it must be said that Christian did not like her sister to be much among Mrs. James's friends. Nor had Mary herself been wont to like it either, but the Mary of a year ago is not the Mary of to-day; she has not grown indifferent to Christian's wishes; very far from that, Mary was perhaps more nervously anxious to please Christian than ever in all lesser things; she felt that a kind of atonement, a satisfaction to her conscience, for her encouragement of the one engrossing feeling of her heart, of which she dared not indeed seek Christian's approval. For the thought that in this most important particular she was deceiving, or at least disingenuous to her dearest friend, concealing from her what it so concerned her to know, gave Mary, acting thus contrary to her nature, many a secret pang. But though this secret clouded her brow and disturbed her peace at home, she hid it in her own heart. Still how strange that Mary should be lightsome and happier with her brother's wife, whose character was in every respect so inferior to her own, than with her gentle sister; yet so it was, and Mary's heart beat quicker when she entered James's house, and quicker still when she saw there was some other visitor before her. Who it was she needed not to ask, for Forsyth sprung to her side, as she entered the cheerful room, with low-voiced salutation, and a glance that brought the blush to her cheek, and caused her fair head to bend over the merry little boy that came running to her knee, and hailed her as "Aunt Mary."

"Call me uncle, James, that's a good little fellow, call me Uncle Walter," said Forsyth.

Mary's blush grew deeper; but James the younger was said to resemble Aunt Christian in many things, and in nothing more than in disliking Forsyth; and he was not to be conciliated, either with sugar-plum or toy, but remained steadfast in his childish instinct of dislike, so he said bluntly, "No,"—a bad omen this; but Forsyth was not to be discouraged, and Mrs. James, nettled a little by it, proceeded at once to open the campaign. Some new music was lying on the table, and she pointed to it.

"See, Mary, here is a present from Mr. Forsyth," she said, laughingly, "but there is a condition attached to it which depends on you for its fulfilment."

Mary, glad of anything to hide her confusion, bent over the table to look at it. "Well," she said, "and what is the condition that depends on me."

"Nay, ask the giver," said Mrs. James, "he must make his agreement with you himself, I cannot make bargains for him."

Mary was half afraid to lift her eyes to Forsyth's face, but she did so, and asked by a glance what it was he required.

"The condition is not a very difficult one," said he, in his most bland and soothing tone, "it was merely that Mrs. Melville would get you to sing this song for me. I was afraid I should fail did I ask myself."

"And why this song, Mr. Forsyth," asked Mary, "is it such a favourite?"

"I heard you sing it a year ago," was the answer, spoken too low, Mary thought, to reach Mrs. James's ear, and again the blood came rushing in torrents to her face.

Mrs. James began to move about as though about to leave the room; this silence would not do, it was too embarrassing, and Mary resumed, though her voice had likewise grown imperceptibly lower. "Christian is very fond of this song, and we all of us like it because she does."

Mrs. James heard this, however, and, elated by Mary's coming to her house that morning, and her own expected triumph over Christian, she could not resist the temptation. "Oh, Christian has such strange notions," she said gaily, "she likes things that nobody else does. I can't conceive why you are all continually quoting Christian—Christian! one hears nothing else from James and you, Mary, but Christian, Christian."

"Christian never set her own inclination in opposition to any other person's wish in her life," said Mary, warmly; "you do not know Christian, Elizabeth, or you would not speak of her so."

"Miss Melville's good qualities," chimed in Forsyth, "Miss Melville's rare qualities, must gain as much admiration wherever she is seen, as they seem to have gotten love and reverence from all who are within the range of their beneficent exercise, and who have the privilege of knowing their value fully;" and he smiled his sweetest smile in Mary's face, as she looked up to him with grateful glistening eyes, and inwardly thanked him for his appreciation of dear Christian in her heart.

How superior, thought Mary, is he to such worldly people as Elizabeth, and her coterie, *he* appreciates Christian, *he* can estimate her properly. Yet Mary, all the time that her heart glowed under these feelings towards Forsyth, felt that she had thwarted Christian's warmest wishes, and is still farther thwarting them by the very look with which she thanked Forsyth for his championship. Mrs. James is at the window carefully examining the leaves of some rare winter plants—another gift of Forsyth's giving; and there ensues another awkward silence. At length she breaks in once more.

"Am I to have my music, Mary? will you fulfil the conditions Mr. Forsyth has attached to this, or shall I have to send it back again?"

Forsyth is leaning over her chair, anxiously waiting for her answer. Mary is at a loss what to do, but cannot say, No. Again Mrs. James is occupied with the flowers.

"This is an era with me, Miss Melville," Forsyth whispered in Mary's ear; "this day twelve months I first saw you."

Mary's fingers still hold the music, but the sheets tremble in her hands. "Is it, indeed?" she says. "Oh, yes! I remember, it was at Elizabeth's annual party! It is an era to us all, also. We too have many recollections connected with the New Year, but they are all sorrowful."

"Not mine," returned Forsyth. "Do you know, Miss Melville, I was much struck then by your resemblance to a young man I once knew in Edinburgh, a very fine gentleman-like lad of your own name too. I often wonder what has become of him. I had some hand in inducing him to change some ridiculously rigid opinions of his; when a fit of superstitious fear came over him, and I believe his regard for me changed to a perfect hatred."

Here Mr. Forsyth looked over to Mrs. James, as much as to say, it was full time for her to go away.

The light is swimming in Mary's eyes, everything before her has become dim and indistinct; and she trembles, not as she trembled a moment since, with agitated pleasure—it is horror, dread, fear that now shakes her slender frame, and looks out from her dim and vacant eyes. There is no trace now of the blush which wavered but a little ago so gracefully upon her cheek, it is pale as death, as she sinks back into her chair. Forsyth and Elizabeth both rushed to her side. What is, what can be, the matter?

"Nothing, nothing, I shall be better immediately," she said, shuddering as she raised herself up again, and drew away the hand which Forsyth had taken; "I am better now, much better."

A look of intelligence and mutual congratulation passed between her companions. Poor thing, she is agitated, and out of sorts with the novelty of her position; but what matters that, they are quite sure of Mary now, and Mrs. James glides quietly out of the room.

As soon as she has gone, and they are left alone together, Forsyth with all the eloquence of look and tone and gesture he can command, pours his suit into Mary's ear. How entirely will he not be devoted to her, to her happiness. How perfectly does she reign in his affections; but it seems, unless from a shiver, which thrills through her frame from time to time, that he speaks to a statue, alike incapable of moving from that charmed place, or of articulating anything in answer to his petition. Forsyth becomes alarmed, and entreats, beseeches her to speak to him, to look at him only, to return the pressure of his hand, if nothing more definite is to be said or done; and suddenly Mary does look up, pale and troubled though her countenance be, into his face, and speaks firmly:—

"Where, Mr. Forsyth," she said, gazing at him as though she could penetrate the veil, and read his inmost heart; "where did that young man go, that you were speaking to me of just now; the one," she added, with hasty irritation, as she marked his astonished and deprecating gesture—"the one you thought resembled me; to what place or country did he flee? Answer me."

"Mary, dear Mary!" pleaded Forsyth, "why ask me such a question now? why terrify me with such looks. That superstitious fellow can be nothing to you; and you, dear Mary, are all in all to me."

Mary's voice is still trembling, notwithstanding her firmness, and the very force of her agitation has made it clear. "Where did he go to?" she repeats once more.

"I do not know; I believe to America, the universal refuge," answered Forsyth, half angrily. "But why do you torment me thus, and answer my entreaties by such questions? What has this to do with my suit? Will you not listen to me, Mary?"

As he spoke, she rose with sudden dignity, and repelled the proud man who subdued and supplicating half knelt before her. "Much, Sir," she said, with emphasis; "it has much to do with what you have said to me. I, to whom you address your love—I, who have been deceived into esteeming you so long— I, am the sister of Halbert Melville; of the man whom your seductions destroyed!"

It is too much, this struggle, the natural feeling will not be restrained, and Mary Melville hides her face in her hands, and tries to keep in the burning tears. Forsyth has been standing stunned, as though a thunderbolt had broken upon his head, but now he starts forward again. She is melting, he thinks, and again he takes her hand in his own. It is forced out of his hold almost fiercely, and Mary, again elevated in transitory strength, bids him begone; she will not look upon the destroyer of her brother with a favourable eye, nor listen to a word from his lips.

A moment after, the passengers in the street are turning round in astonishment, to look at that face so livid with rage and disappointment which speeds past them like a flash of lightning, and Mrs. James Melville was called up to administer restoratives to her fainting sister—sweet gentle Mary.

CHAPTER III.

If I may trust the flattering eye of sleep,
My dreams presage some joyful news at hand;
My bosom's lord sits lightly in his throne;
And, all this day, an unaccustom'd spirit
Lifts me above the ground with cheerful thoughts.
Romeo and Juliet.

CHRISTIAN MELVILLE is seated alone by her fireside, engaged in her usual occupations, and full of her wonted thoughts; but her present anxiety about Mary has taught her to linger less in the past, and to look oftener forward to the future than she has been accustomed to do heretofore, since sorrow made that once bright prospect a blank to her. Nay, Christian, in her happier hours, has grown a dreamer of dreams, and all her architectural fancies terminate in the one grand object, the happiness of Mary. She sees the imminent danger she runs of having to relinquish her one remaining treasure, and that into the keeping of one she distrusts so much as Forsyth. Christian cannot tell how it is that she has such an unaccountable, unconquerable aversion to him. True, his name is the same as that of Halbert's tempter; and association is the root, doubtless, of all her prejudice—as prejudice everybody calls it—and Christian tries, as she has tried a hundred times, to overcome her repugnance, and to recollect the good traits of character that have been told her of him, and to school her mind into willingness to receive him as Mary's choice; and she breathes, from the depths of her heart, the fervent petition for guidance and deliverance so often repeated for her innocent Mary—her child, her sister—and then her thoughts speed away, and Halbert rises up before her mental vision. What can be his fate? Long and wearily does she ponder, and bitter fancies often make her groan in spirit as one burdened. Is he still a living man?—still to be hoped and prayed for; or, is Halbert now beyond all human hope and intercession? Her heart grows sick and faint as she thinks of the possibility of this; but she almost instantly rejects it; and again her soul rises to her Lord in earnest ejaculations. Oh! but for this power of prayer, but for this well-ascertained certainty, that there is One who hears the prayers of his people, how should Christian Melville have lived throughout these three long anxious years; how should she have endured the unbroken monotony of every uneventful day, with such a load upon her mind, and such fancies coming and going in her heart; how possibly subdued the longings of her anxious love through all this time of waiting and suspense? But her prayer has never ceased; like the smoke of the ancient sacrifice, it has ascended continually through the distant heaven: the voice of her supplications and intercedings have risen up without ceasing; and surely the Hearer of prayer will not shut his ears to these.

There is some commotion going on below, the sound of which comes up to Christian in a confused murmur, in which she can only distinguish old Ailie's voice. At first she takes no notice of it; then she begins to wonder what it can be, so strange are such sounds in this quiet and methodical house, though still she does not rise to inquire what it is. Christian is engrossed too much with her own thoughts; and as the sounds grow more indistinct, she bends her head again, and permits herself to be carried away once more in the current of her musings. But the step of old Ailie is coming up the stairs much more rapidly than that old footstep was wont to come; and as Christian looks up again in astonishment, Ailie rushes into the room, spins round it for a moment with uplifted hands, sobbing and laughing mingled, in joyful confusion, and then dropping on the floor, breathless and exhausted with her extraordinary pirouetting, throws her apron over her head, and weeps and laughs, and utters broken ejaculations till Christian, hastening across the room in great alarm to interrogate her, afraid that the old woman's brain is affected,

"What is the matter, Ailie?" Christian asks. "Tell me, what is the matter?"

"Oh, Miss Christian!" and poor Ailie's wail of sobbing mixed with broken laughter sounded almost unearthly in Christian's ear. "Oh, Miss Christian! said I not, that the bairn of sae monie prayers suld not be lost at last?"

"Ailie! Ailie! what do you mean? Have you heard anything of Halbert?" and Christian trembled like a leaf, and could scarce speak her question for emotion. "Ailie! I entreat you to speak to—to answer me."

And Christian wrung her hands in an agony of hope and fear, unwitting what to think or make of all this almost hysterical emotion of the old faithful servant, or of her enigmatical words. "Look up, dear Christian; look up!" Ailie needs not answer. Who is this that stands on the threshold of this well-remembered room, with a flush of joy on his cheek, and a shade of shame and fearfulness just tempering the glow of happiness in his eyes?

"Halbert!"

"Christian!"

The brother and sister so fearfully and so long separated, and during these years unwitting of each other's existence even, are thus restored to each other once more.

A long story has Halbert to tell, when Christian has recovered from her first dream of confused joy, a three year long story, beginning with that fearful night, the source of all his sorrows and his sufferings. Christian's heart is bent down in silent shuddering horror as he tells her of how he fell; how he was seduced, as by the craftiness of an Ahithophel, into doubt, into scoffing, into avowed unbelief, and finally led by his seducer—who all the previous time had seemed pure and spotless as an angel of light—into the haunts of his profligate associates, so vicious, so degrading, that the blush mantles on Halbert's cheek at the bare remembrance of that one night. He tells her how among them he was led to acknowledge the change which Forsyth had wrought upon his opinions, and how he had been welcomed as one delivered from the bondage of priestly dreams and delusions; how he was taken with them when they left Forsyth's house—the host himself the prime leader and chief of all—and saw scenes of evil which he shuddered still to think of; and how in the terrible revulsion of his feelings which followed his first knowledge of the habits of these men, whose no-creed he had adopted, and whose principles he had openly confessed the night before, sudden and awful conviction laid hold upon him—conviction of the nature of sin; of his sin in chief—and an apprehension of the hopelessness of pardon being extended to him; and how, turning reckless in his despair, he had resolved to flee to some place where he was unknown, uncaring what became of himself. He told her then of his long agony, of his fearful struggle with despair, which engrossed his soul, and how at last he was prompted by an inward influence to the use of the means of grace once more; and how, when at length he dared to open his Bible again, a text of comfort and of hopefulness looked him in the face; that he had said to himself, over and over again, "It is impossible!" till hope had died in his heart: but here this true word contradicted at once the terrible utterance of his self-abandonment. "All things," it was written, "are possible with God;" and Halbert told her, how the first tears that had moistened his eyes since his great fall sprang up in them that very day. He told her of the scene so fair, where this mighty utterance of the Almighty went to his soul, and where he found peace; in the words of the gifted American—

"Oh, I could not choose but go
Into the woodlands hoar.

"Into the blithe and breathing air,
Into the solemn wood,
Solemn and silent everywhere!
Nature with folded arms seem'd there,
Kneeling at her evening prayer!
Like one in prayer I stood.

"Before me rose an avenue
Of tall and sombrous pines;

Abroad their fanlike branches grew,
And where the sunshine darted through,
Spread a vapour soft and blue.
In long and sloping lines.

"And falling on my weary brain,
Like a fast falling shower,
The dreams of youth came back again;
Low lispings of the summer rain,
Dropping on the ripen'd grain,
As once upon the flower."

He told her of his happy progress, from that first dawning of hope to the full joy of steadfast faith. He ran over the history of the past year, in which from day to day he had looked forward to this meeting; and he told with what joy he had slowly added coin to coin, until he had saved a sufficient sum to carry him home. Then, when he had finished, the sister and brother mingled their thanksgivings and happiness together, and Christian's heart swelled full and overbrimming: she could have seated herself upon the floor, like Ailie, and poured out her joy as artlessly. But it is Halbert's turn now to ask questions. When will little Mary be home? how long she stays. Halbert wearies to see his little sister, but he is bidden remember that she is not little now, and Christian sighs, and the dark cloud, that she fears is hanging over Mary's fate, throws somewhat of its premonitory gloom upon her heart and face. Halbert, unnoticing this, is going about the room, almost like a boy, looking lovingly at its well-remembered corners, and at the chairs and tables, at the books, and last his eye falls on a card lying in a little basket, and he starts as if he had encountered a serpent, and his eye flashes as he suddenly cries out, almost sternly, as he lifts it and reads the name.

"Christian, what is this—what means this? Mr. Walter Forsyth a visitor of yours; it cannot be. Tell me, Christian, what does it mean?"

"It is Mr. Forsyth's card," said Christian gravely; "an acquaintance, I am afraid I must say a *friend* of ours. Indeed, Halbert, now that you are home with us again, this is my only grief. I fear we shall have to give our little Mary into his keeping, and he is not worthy of her."

Halbert is calmed by his long trial, but his natural impetuosity is not entirely overcome, and he starts up in sudden excitement and disorder. "Walter Forsyth the husband of my sister Mary! Walter Forsyth, the infidel, the profligate; better, Christian, better a thousand times, that we should lay her head in the grave, great trial as that would be, and much agony as it would cause us all, than permit her to unite herself with such a reptile."

"Halbert," said Christian, "the name misleads you; this cannot be the man—the Forsyth who wrought you so much unhappiness and harm, and has caused us all such great grief and sorrow; he must be much older, and altogether a different person. This one is not even a scoffer, at least so far as I have seen."

"Christian," cried Halbert vehemently, "I feel assured it is the same. Do not tell me what he pretends to be, if he has any end to serve he can be anything, and put on the seeming of an angel of light even. I tell you, Christian, that I am sure, quite sure, that it *is* he. I met him as I came here, and I shuddered as I saw him, and even felt myself shrinking back lest his clothes should touch me; but little did I suspect that he was about to bring more grief upon us. Does Mary, do you think, care for him?"

Christian could not but tell him her fears; but she said also that Mary had always avoided speaking to her on the subject. What could they do? What should be done to save Mary? Halbert, in his impatience, would have gone to seek her out at once, and have pointed out to her the character of her lover; but Christian only mournfully shook her head, such a plan was most likely to do harm and not good.

"You must be calm, Halbert," she said, "this impetuosity will be injurious—we must save Mary by gentler means, she is far too like yourself to be told in this outspoken manner—the shock would kill her."

But old Ailie is stealing the door of the room open timidly, to break in on the first hour of Christian's joy, and when she entered she did it with a look of sober cheerfulness, widely different from her late joyful frenzy.

"Miss Mary came in a while since," she said, "and ran straight up to her own room, without speaking, or waiting till I telled her of Mr. Halbert's home coming, and she looked pale and ill like; would you not go up, Miss Christian, and see?"

The Melvilles are Ailie's own children, and she has a mother's care of them in all their troubles, bodily or mental. So at her bidding Christian rose and went softly to Mary's room: the door was closed, but she opened it gently, and standing hidden by the curtains of Mary's bed, was witness to the wild burst of passionate sorrow and disappointed affection in which Mary's breaking heart gushed forth, when she found herself once more alone. Herself unseen, Christian saw the scalding tears welling out from her gentle sister's dim and swollen eyes, she saw the convulsive motions of her lithe and graceful figure, as she rocked herself to and fro, as if to ease or still the burning grief within: and she heard her broken murmurs.

"Had he but died before I knew this, I would have mourned for him all my life, even as Christian mourns, but now—but now!—such as he is"—and her burst of sobbing checked the voice of her sorrow. A moment after she started up and dashed the tears from her eyes, with some vehemence. "Should I not rather thank God that I have been saved from uniting myself with a godless man—with my poor brother's seducer?" and she sank on her knees by the bedside. Poor Mary's grief was too great for silent supplications, and Christian stood entranced, as that prayer, broken by many a gush of weeping, rose through the stillness of the quiet room. She had never, she thought, heard such eloquence before of supplicating sorrow, had never seen the omnipotence of truth and faith till then; gradually they seemed to subdue and overcome the wildness of that first grief, gradually attuned that sweet young sobbing, struggling voice, to sweetest resignation, and ere Christian echoed the solemn "Amen," Mary had given thanks for her deliverance, though still natural tears, not to be repressed, broke in on her thanksgiving, and silent weeping followed her ended prayer. But when she bent her head upon her hands again, Christian's kind arm was around her, Christian's tears were mingled with her own, Christian's lips were pressed to her wet cheek in tender sympathy, and the voice of Christian, like a comforter, whispered,

"I know all, Mary, I know all; may God strengthen you, my dear sister—you have done nobly, and as you should have done; may God bless you, dearest Mary."

And Mary's head, as in her old childish sorrows, nestles on Christian's bosom, and Mary's heart is relieved of half its heavy and bitter load. Poor Mary! the days of childhood have indeed come back again, and, as the violence of the struggle wears away, she weeps herself to sleep, for sorrow has worn out the strength of her delicate frame, already exhausted by the varied and contending emotions of the day, and now the tears slide slowly from beneath her closed eyelids even in her sleep.

But Halbert is at the door anxiously begging for admittance, and Christian leads him in to look at little Mary's sleep. It was a child's face, the last time he looked upon it, a happy girlish face, where mirth and quick intelligence rivalled each other in bringing out its expressive power; he sees it now, a woman's, worn with the first and sorest struggle that its loving nature could sustain, and a kind of reverence mingled with his warm affection as he bent over his sleeping sister; *he* had yielded to temptations, oh, how much weaker, since his heart was not enlisted on the tempter's side; *he* had made shipwreck of his faith and of his peace, for years, fascinated by attractions a thousand times less potent than those which this girl, her slight figure still trembling with her late emotions, still weeping in her sleep, had withstood and overcome; and Halbert bent his head, humility mingling with his rejoicing. Had he only been as steadfast as Mary, how much sorrow and suffering would they all have been saved.

They have left the room awhile with quiet footsteps, and there is much gladness in those two hearts, though trembling still mingles with their joy; for, if Christian fears the effect of this terrible shock on Mary's health, at least she is delivered; there is great happiness in that certainty, she has found out Forsyth's true character, though it passes all their guessing and conjectures to tell how.

And now Halbert is asking about his father, and James and Robert, and expressing his fears as to how they will receive him, the truant son. His brothers will be rejoiced; but Christian shakes her head half doubtful, half smiling, when Halbert, "and my father"—she cannot say, but an hour or two more will bring that to the proof.

"Do you know, Christian, I feel myself like one of the broken men of the old ballads, and I am in doubt, in perplexity, and fear, about this meeting."

"If you are broken, if your ship has been cast ashore, we will get it mended again," said Christian, with more of humour and lightheartedness than she had either felt or used for many a day. "But no more of that, Halbert, just now. Tell me, will you go to see James to-night?"

"No, I can't; it would be unseemly besides."

Halbert will not leave his sister the first night of his return, and Christian feels relieved; after a pause, he continues:

"How do you like Elizabeth now, Christian; are James and she happy together?"

"I have no doubt they are," said Christian, evasively; "why should they not be?"

"But you don't like her."

"I never said so, Halbert."

"Well, that's true enough; but I inferred it."

"Nay, you must make no inferences. Elizabeth can be very pleasant and lovable; if she is not always so, it is but because she does not choose to exercise her powers of pleasing."

"So she can be lovable when she likes. But it was she, was it not, that introduced Mary to Forsyth?" said Halbert, his brow darkening.

"You must forgive her that, Halbert; she was not aware of his character when she received him as her cousin's friend," and Christian looked distressed and uneasy, and continued; "and Halbert, you must not cherish a vindictive feeling even against Forsyth, bad as he is, and great as is the mischief he did you; promise me that, Halbert, promise me, now."

"Well, I do promise you; I could not, if I would; and I now pity him much more than hate him."

They sat together conversing, till the shadows began to lengthen, when Christian, compelled by domestic cares and preparations for the evening, left her new found brother for a time.

CHAPTER IV.

Bear a lily in thy hand;
Gates of brass cannot withstand
One touch of that magic wand.

Bear through sorrow, wrong and ruth,
In thy heart the dew of youth,
On thy lips the smile of truth.—LONGFELLOW.

THE day wore away, and now the evening darkened fast, and old Ailie's beaming face, illuminated by the lights she carries, interrupts brother and sister, again seated in the cheerful fire-light, which, ere the candles are set upon the table, has filled the room with such a pleasant flickering half-gloom, half-radiance. And there, too, is Mr. Melville's knock, which never varies, at the door. Halbert knows it as well as Christian, and grows pale and involuntarily glides into a corner—as he had done of old when he had transgressed—but Christian has met her father at the door, and whispered that there is a stranger newly arrived in the room. It fortunately so happens to-night that Mr. Melville has come home more complacent and willing to be pleased than he has done for many a day. Some speculation suggested by James, and agreed to with sundry prudent demurring by the heads of the house, has turned out most successfully, and Mr. Melville has taken the credit of James's foresight and energy all to himself, and is marvellously pleased therewith. "A stranger, aye, Christian, and who is this stranger?" he says most graciously, as he divests himself of his outer wrappings; but Christian has no voice to answer just then, and so he pushes open the half-shut door, and looks curiously about the room; his son stands before him, his eyes cast down, his cheeks flushed, his heart beating.

"Halbert!"

The human part of Mr. Melville's nature melts for the moment, the surprise is pleasurable; but he soon grows stern again.

"Where have you been, sir? what have you been doing? and why have you never written to your sister?"

Halbert's trial has taught him meekness, and his answers are in words which turn away wrath, and his father turns round to seek his easy-chair on the most sheltered and cosiest side of the glowing fire.

"Humph!" he says; "well, since you are home, I suppose it's no use making any more enquiries now, but what do you intend to do?"

Halbert looks astonished; it is a question he is not prepared to answer; he feels that he ought not and cannot ask his father to enable him to carry out the plan he has been dreaming of for the past twelve months, and he is silent.

"There is plenty of time for answering that, father," said Christian briskly; "we can consult about that afterwards, when we have all recovered ourselves a little from this surprise which Halbert has given us; and here comes Robert."

Robert came merrily into the room as Christian spoke, and not alone, he had a companion with him whom he brought forward to introduce to Christian, when his eye caught his brother. What! are we going to have old Ailie's extravagances over again. Poor Robert's laugh is hysterical as he tumbles over half a dozen chairs, and lays hold of Halbert, and his shout electrifies the whole household, wakening poor sleeping Mary in her lonely chamber. "Halbert! Halbert"—Robert is a fine fellow for all his thoughtlessness, and is almost weeping over his recovered brother, and Halbert's newly acquired composure has forsaken him again, and he sobs and grasps Robert's hands, and thanks God in his heart. This is truly a prodigal's welcome, which Halbert feels he deserves not.

Robert's companion hangs back bashfully, unwilling to break in upon, lest he mar this scene of heartfelt family joy, which a good brother like himself fully appreciates; but Christian's kind and watchful eye is upon him, and has marked him, and she comes forward to relieve him from the awkward position in which he is placed, Marked him! yes, but what a startled agitated look it is with which she regards him, and seems to peruse every lineament of his countenance with eager earnestness. What can it be that comes thus in the way of Christian's considerate courtesy, and makes her retire again and gaze and wonder? What a resemblance! and Christian's heart beats quick. But Robert has at length recollected himself, and now brings the young man forward and introduces him as his friend Charles Hamilton. Christian returns his greeting, but starts again and exchanges a hurried glance with Halbert, who also looks wonderingly on the stranger. Christian soon leaves the room, she has Mary to seek after, and attend to; but as she passes Halbert's chair, she bends over it and whispers in his ear, and her voice trembles the while,—

"Is not the resemblance most striking—and the name?"

"It is most extraordinary," answered Halbert aloud, gazing again on the mild ingenuous face of the stranger. Christian glided away.

"What is most extraordinary, Halbert?" asked Robert, with a slight impatience in his tone.

"Oh, nothing; at least only Mr. Hamilton's great resemblance to an old friend of ours long since dead."

The young man looked towards him and smiled. Can that picture still be hanging in its old place in Christian's room?

Our poor Mary has slept long and calmly, and when Robert's shout awoke her, she started up in astonishment. She was lying in the dark room alone, with silence round about her, and her pillow was wet with tears. Mary raised herself in her bed, and throwing back the disordered hair which hung about her face tried to collect her bewildered thoughts. The memory of her grief has left her for the moment, and she is wondering what the sound could be that came indistinctly to her ears; it sounded, she fancied, very like "Halbert." Who could be speaking of him, and as she repeats his name the full knowledge of what has passed, all the momentous events and misery of this day come upon her like a dream. Poor Mary! a heavy sigh breaks from her parted lips, and she presses her hand over her painful eyes. She does not see the approaching light which steals into the little room; she does not hear the light footstep of its gentle bearer, but she feels the kind pressure of Christian's arm, and most readily and thankfully rests her head on Christian's supporting shoulder.

"I have news to tell you," whispers Christian, "which you will be glad of and smile at, though you are sighing now. You remember Halbert, Mary?"

Remember him! but Mary's only answer is a sigh. Halbert's name has terrible associations for her to-night; she has remembered him and his fortunes so well and clearly this day.

"Mary, Halbert has come home, will you rouse yourself to see him?"

"Come home, Halbert come home!" and the poor girl lifted up her head. "Forgive me, Christian, forgive me, but I have done very wrong, and I am very, very unhappy;" and the tears flowed on Christian's neck again more freely than before.

"You have done nobly, dear Mary—only rouse yourself, shake off this grief; you have done well, and God will give you strength. Let me bathe your temples—you will soon be better now," said Christian, parting the long dishevelled hair, and wiping away the still streaming tears. "That man is not worthy one tear from you, Mary: be thankful rather, dearest, for your deliverance from his cunning and his wiles."

A deep blush flitted over Mary's tear-stained face, as she raised herself and began with Christian's tender assistance to remove the traces of her grief. Christian wondered as she saw her begin to move about the little room again; there was a still composure gathering about her gentle features, which the elder sister, accustomed to think of Mary as still little more than a child, could only marvel at in silence. Her eyes were almost stern in their calmness, and her voice was firmer than Christian could have believed possible as she turned to speak.

"Yes, Christian, I am thankful—thankful beyond anything I can say; but do not ask me about anything just now," she continued, hurriedly, as Christian looked up to her as if about to speak. "I will tell you all afterwards, but not to-night—not to-night, dear Christian."

"Would you not like to see Halbert, Mary?" said Christian, taking the cold hands of her sister in her own. "Do you care or wish to see Halbert now, Mary?"

"Yes, yes," was the answer, and Mary's eye assumed a kinder and more natural glow. "I forgot, tell him to come here Christian, I would rather see him, I cannot meet him down stairs."

Halbert was speedily summoned, and when his step paused at the door, Mary ran forward to meet him with pleasure in her eyes. True, Halbert's tone of affectionate sympathy brought the remembrance of that scene of the morning, and with it the tears to Mary's eyes; but Christian rejoiced to see how gently they fell, and hoped that the sorest and bitterest part of the struggle was past; and so it was, for Mary went down with untrembling step and entered the room where her father, brother, and the stranger sat with a sweet and settled calmness, which allayed all Christian's fears.

It seemed now that however strange the stranger was to Christian, he was no stranger to Mary Melville. Mr. Charles Hamilton was in truth well known to Mary—yea, that Robert looked arch and intelligent, and his young friend blushed as he rose to greet her on her entrance. This acquaintanceship was soon explained, Mary had met him several times at Mrs. James's parties, and the casual mention which Robert and Mary had made of him among the host of Elizabeth's visitors had not been sufficiently marked to attract the attention of Christian, engrossed as she was then with such great anxiety regarding poor Mary's unfortunate attachment.

Charles Hamilton's qualities of head and heart were much too *large* for Mrs. James Melville, and, accordingly, though she received him as a guest, and was even glad to do so, from his social position and prospects—she regarded him with much the same feeling which prompted her attacks on Christian, and having noticed what poor Mary was too much occupied to notice, the bashful attention with which the young man hovered about her fair sister-in-law, Mrs. James had decided upon entirely crushing his hopes by exhibiting to him this evening, at her party, the crowning triumph of her friend Forsyth. Poor Mrs. James! how completely she had over-reached and outwitted herself. That evening found her accomplished friend the rejected—rejected with scorn and loathing, too—of simple Mary Melville, in no humour for contributing to the amusement of her guests, and Charles Hamilton in a far fairer way of success than even he himself had ever dreamt of, for Christian's eyes are bent on him from time to time, and there is wonder blended with kindness in her frequent glances on his face, and her pleasant voice has an unconscious tone of affection in it as she speaks to him, as though she were addressing a younger brother. But the time has come when they must prepare for Mrs. James's party; Christian will not go, Mary will not go, how could she? Halbert will not go, and the young stranger's face grows suddenly clouded, and he moves uneasily on his chair, and at last rises reluctantly. Mr. Melville and Robert must go for a time at least, to excuse the others that remain at home, and tell James of Halbert's return, and Charles Hamilton in vain hunts through every recess of his inventive powers to find some reason that will excuse him for sitting down again. But all fail, he can find nothing to offer as an excuse; he is intruding on the family this night, sacred as it is—the evening of the wanderer's return—and when he may suppose they all so much desire to be alone; and so he must take his leave, however loth and reluctant so to do. But while so perplexed and disappointed Christian takes him aside, Christian bids him sit down and speak to her a moment when Robert and his father have gone away, and he does so gladly. Mary wonders what Christian can have to say to him, a stranger to her till the last hour, and looks over, with interest every moment increasing, towards the corner where they are seated side by side, and so does Halbert too; but there is no astonishment in his face, though there is compassionate affection beaming from his eyes. Their conversation seems to be most interesting to both, and the look of sad recollection on Christian's gentle face seems to have been communicated to the more animated features of her companion, and at length he suddenly starts and clasps her hand.

"Christian Melville!" he exclaims, "Oh that my mother were here!"

The tears stand in Christian's eyes—some chord of old recollection has been touched more powerfully than usual, and Christian's cheeks are wet, and her eyes cast down for a moment. Mary can only gaze in astonishment, and before she recovers herself Christian has led the young man forward to them, and then she hurries from the room, while Halbert extends his hand to him cordially. What is the meaning of this? both the young men join in explanations, but Charles Hamilton's voice is broken, half with the recollection of his dead brother, and half with the pleasure of discovering such a tie already existing with Mary's family. Yes, Charles's brother was the original of that saint-like portrait which hangs within reach of the glories of sunset on the wall of Christian's room. The grave where Christian had buried her youthful hopes was the grave of William Hamilton, and that one name made the young man kindred to them all; and when Christian after a time came down stairs again, she found him seated between Halbert and Mary as though he had been familiar with that fireside circle all his days, and was indeed a brother.

It was a happy night that to the group in this bright room, a night of great cheerfulness and pleasant communion, just heightened by the saddening tinge which memory gave it, and Mary, our sweet Mary, marvels at herself, and is half disappointed that there is so little of romance in the fading of her sorrow; but marvel as she likes, the unwitting smile plays on her lips again, and you could scarce believe that those clear eyes have shed so many tears to-day. She feels easier and happier even, now the weight of concealment, which disturbed and distressed her in Christian's presence of late, is removed from the spirit; and she is the same open, single-minded, ingenuous girl as heretofore; the secret consciousness that it was not right to yield to Forsyth's fascinating powers is gone now, and Mary Melville is herself once more, aye, more herself than she has been for months past, notwithstanding the bitter suffering of that very day. God has graciously tempered the fierceness of his wind to the tender and trembling lamb, and Christian's confidence is restored, and she feels sure that time will make Mary's heart as light as ever, and efface from her memory the image of that evil man, and blot out the traces of this day's agony; and a smile flits over Christian's cheerful face as she fancies the substitution of another image in the precious entablature of Mary's heart. Who can tell but Charles Hamilton may gain a right to the name of brother, which she already hesitates not to accord, better than his present claim, precious to her mind as it is.

Mrs. James Melville's party is sadly shorn of its lustre this year, when we compare it with its last predecessor, only a short twelvemonth since; and already, in spite of all the attractions of gossip, music, and flirtation, her guests are beginning to yawn and look weary. Mrs. James was never so annoyed in her life, all seems this night to have gone wrong. Her very husband had deserted her—she had seen him fly down stairs three steps at a time, and skim away through the cold street towards his father's house. Mrs. James was enraged to be left alone at such a time for any Halbert of them all.

"A nice fuss was made about him, as much nonsense when he went away as if there wasn't another in the whole country, and now when he thought fit and had come home——"

Mrs. James could not finish the sentence, for spite and vexation overmastered her. Forsyth was not there, her chief attraction; Mary was not there, and even Christian's absence, little as she liked her, was another source of annoyance; and this flying off of James was the finishing stroke. We hardly think, however, that even Mrs. James would not have melted had she seen her husband in the middle of yon cheerful group, with his beaming joyous face, shaking Halbert's hands over and over again, to the imminent danger of bone and joint. We really think she could not but have helped him.

There was a voice of thanksgiving in Mr. Melville's house that night, of thanksgiving which told in its earnest acknowledgment of many mercies; thanksgiving whose voice was broken by the sobbings of one and accompanied by the happy tears of all, for Halbert led their devotions, and when his earnest tones rose up among them there was not a dry cheek in the kneeling family, not James, though it might be thought his heart was alienated from the overflowing affection of home, by the remembrance of his own; not Charles Hamilton, permitted, nay requested, to stay, for who so well as Halbert could give thanks for that double deliverance.

There are dreams to-night hovering with drowsy wing about the dwelling, dreams which alight on Charles Hamilton's young head as he hastens home, his heart full of the last scene of the evening, and his voice repeating—

"In dwellings of the righteous
Is heard the melody
Of joy and health: the Lord's right hand
Doth ever valiantly;"—

dreams which enter Halbert Melville's long shut chamber, welcoming its old dreamer back again—dreams which float about Christian's resting-place—above the fair head laid on Christian's shoulder, calm as in the happy days of childhood; sweet, hopeful, cheering dreams, that open up long vistas of indistinct and dazzling brightness, all the brighter for their glad uncertainty before their eyes, and fill the hearts which tremble in their joy with a sweet assurance that calms their fears into peace. Even Ailie dreamed, and her visions were of a gay complexion, fitting the nature of her doings through this eventful day, and had various anticipations of bridal finery floating through them. Nay, the very wind which whistled past Mr. Melville's roof-tree had a language of its own, and admirable gleesome chuckle, which said plain as words could speak that happy as this night had been beneath it, there would be merrier, happier doings here next new year's day.

EPOCH V.

Sweet is the sunshine lacing with its light,
The parting storm-cloud after day of sadness;
That ere the even darkens into night
O'erflows the world with glory and with gladness;
But sweeter is the flood of pleasantness,
That breaks at noonday through the clouds of morning,
While yet the long glad hours have power to bless,
And the earth brightens 'neath its warm adorning
Of scattered sunbeams. So their fate excels
In blessedness, upon whose noonday story
The heavenly sunshine of God's favour dwells,
While yet their tongues are strong to speak His glory;
And blessed they, O Lord! who, saved and free,
Stretch out compassionate hands to draw men near to thee!

CHAPTER I.

They thicken on our path,
These silent witness years;
A solemn tenantry, that still land hath
Wherein were spent our bygone smiles and tears;
Graven on their secret tablets silently,
Stand deed, and thought, and word,
Beyond the touch of change or soft decay,
'Stablished perpetually before the Lord!
*   *   *   *   *
Season of labour, time of hope and fear,
Kind to our households let thy varyings be;
With thee we give a sigh to the Old year,
And do rejoice us in the New with thee.—Y.S.P.

TEN years have passed away, and again it is a fireside scene that we have to depict, and a fireside conversation we have to chronicle. The room we now stand in is large and pleasant, and bright with the radiance of merry faces— faces of every age and size, but all marvellously alike in features, as in happiness, from the grave seniors down to the crowing baby, through all the gradations of stature and sobriety that crowd around that well-spread table. The assembly is too large, and the children too near each other in age to allow you to think them all members of one household; and two fathers half checked, half encouraged the merry crowd, and two mothers took sweet counsel together, praising each other's little ones, and exchanging domestic experiences with each other. We must try and find in these merry faces the traits of those we have known before. Let us see whom we have before us. A man of goodly presence is the elder; grave, it seems, habitually, but with a smile that is like a sunbeam, and which has an electrical effect in the saddest house it beams in; and many, many houses of sorrow does it see, and many mourners are cheered by the words of hope and comfort that flow from these sympathising lips; for you will see, if you look at his apparel, and mark his manner, that he holds a high vocation, no less than a labourer about that glorious vine which has the Eternal Father for its husbandman; a labourer, one who, like the bee, seeks honey from every flower, and from his pulpit, and standing by beds of suffering, and in the dark, close, and fœtid haunts of sin, seeks to have souls for his hire as the labour of his life and the joy of his existence. No mere Sabbath day worker in his pulpit, but one that never tires, that is always ready, and almost always with his harness on his back; like a good knight of the olden time, prompt to succour the distressed. The lady too, who sits beside him, has about her a gentle dignity that is akin to his; but with her blooming cheek and bright eye we can boast no old acquaintance, though when she lays her white hand on his arm and calls him "Halbert," we are half ashamed to say so much of Halbert Melville's wife.

But on the other side of the fire sits a younger lady, with a calm air of matronly self-possession, which almost sets our memory at defiance; it is true that her face looks so youthful in its eloquent expressiveness that, but for that copy of it that shines at her knee, through the fair straggling locks of a little merry girl, you might fancy her still the Mary of ten years ago; but in the silent depths of her dark eyes sits such serene and assured happiness, at once so calm, and deep, and full, as makes one sure this cannot be the disconsolate inhabitant of yon dim chamber, weeping in her sleep in the first agony of womanly woe. Yet so it is, and lightly have these ten swift years—long, oh, how long and dreary to many—flown over her, effacing so entirely everything but the remembrance of those passages in her history from her mind, that when she looks back now upon that troubled time, she half smiles, half blushes for her old self, and reckons of her brief but agonising trial, as sick men recall to their memories the terrible dreams of some delirious fever fit. For Mary Melville has found entire and perfect kindred in the heart of one whom then she little recked of and cared not for, and she wonders now how she, ever the object of Charles Hamilton's warm and full affection, could have overlooked his nobler qualities, and preferred instead Forsyth's deceptive and hollow brilliancy, and the glitter of well-displayed accomplishments, which threw the blushing youth into the shade. And the blushing youth of our last chapter blushes no longer when he speaks to Mary, nor has his bashfulness been seen, Halbert says, for nine long years and more; never since one bright autumn evening, when Mary and he surprised Christian in her solitude by the whispered communication of an important agreement come to between them, and which was carried into effect, ratified and sealed, on the following new year's day, fulfilling, in the most joyous manner, old Ailie's dream. At this transaction Halbert's presence was indispensable, albeit he was again, after Christian's kind persuasions and James's spirited remonstrances had shamed their father into liberality, finishing the long forsaken studies so disastrously interrupted of old, with a vigour and ardour that was unquenchable. True, he did not come to James's wedding when it took place; but Christian, and Mary, and Charles Hamilton were each and all immovable in their demands; they could not do without Halbert, and so he was present at the ceremony, exciting Charles's wrathful contradiction, and Christian and Mary's curiosity, by hinting merrily of another Mary, whose presence would throw the bride of to-day into the shade, though no one at that blithe bridal looked on Mary Melville with more affectionate admiration than her brother Halbert. And lo! when the time of Halbert's study and probations was over, and Providence had so ordered that the place of his ministry should be the same as that of his birth, and the dwelling-place still of his nearest and dearest kindred, then came about another bridal, and the name of Mary Melville was resuscitated, though Mrs. Charles Hamilton's proud husband would never allow that the old bearer of the name was equalled by the new.

But there is no rivalship between the sisters—sisters in affection as much as in name—and the children, whose fair heads have sprung up like flowers beside and about them, are like one family in their cordial intercourse. But where is Christian? Our enquiry is echoed by half-a-dozen merry voices. "Where can Aunt Christian be?" There will be no need to ask the question a moment hence, if indeed we can discern our old friend through the pyramid of children that are clustering about her; the little girl that stood by Mary's knee has left for Aunt Christian, and now stands on a chair beside her, with her round arms about her neck, and her rosy face beaming on her shoulders; the sturdy boy who leant on Halbert's chair has left that place of honour for Aunt Christian, and he stands proudly at her right hand as prime minister, helping at the distribution of the great basketful of new year's dainties—for this is again the first night of another year—which she has brought to gladden these youthful hearts. The whole host of her nephews and nieces, absorbed a moment since in their various amusements, have left them all for Aunt Christian, and are gathered about her, one clinging round her waist and one hanging at either arm, greatly impeding the action of her gift-dispensing hand. Sure enough here is Christian, how blithe! how happy! Time has dealt gently with her, and though he has drawn a thread of silver through the rich dark abundance of her plainly braided hair, there is not one in this room that would not start up in indignant surprise, if you said that Christian was either looking or growing old.

"Nay, nay," said Halbert, not long ago, when some indifferent friend of the family suggested this, "Christian will never grow old. When years come upon her, she will glide away like a streamlet into a river, but she will not fade. Christian's spirit will always be young."

And so it is; her soft clear voice stills all that little childish hubbub in a moment. The very baby stays its scream of joy, as if it too would listen to Aunt Christian, and little Mary on her shoulder, and strong Halbert at her right hand, and every separate individual of their respective hosts of brothers and sisters would dare in single-handed valour any full-grown Goliath that would presume to interrupt the expression of Aunt Christian's pleasure, pleasant as it always is. It is a great day this, with these two united families. A day of childish jubilee to the younger members, and of joyful commemoration to the older, for Halbert looks back with glistening eyes, and rejoices in the union of ten years ago, a beginning of happy, laborious years to him; and Mary remembers her early trial, and thanks God most earnestly for deliverance, and participates with her husband in the happier recollections of their marriage day; and the other Mary, with generous affection, sympathises with each and all; and Christian? Christian's heart, open at all times to generous impulses, seems to have its sluices of overpouring and constant love thrown wide open for the free passage of its swelling tides, each new year's night, and if you heard her fervent thanksgiving when she kneels before God alone, you would think that flood of blessings had been all poured out upon her, not that its fulness had flowed upon her friends, but that she herself was the individual recipient of every separate gift. For Christian identifies herself with those dear ones so entirely, that she looks upon their happiness as a peculiar blessing bestowed upon herself. Christian has, however, now seated herself in the empty chair waiting for her—jealously kept for her, indeed—at the brightest corner of the cheerful fireside, and taking a little namesake of her own, a grave, serious, thoughtful child, who has begun to lisp wisdom already with her infant tongue, upon her knee, she joins in the conversation which her entrance, and still more her equitable distribution of the basket of good things had interrupted.

"Father," questioned Halbert Melville, second bearer of the name, "do you keep new year's day because *it is* new year's day?"

"Why do you ask, Halbert?" said his mother, smiling, as she drew the boy towards her.

"Because, Mamma, nobody else cares about it here; and I've heard Aunt Christian say how foolish it was for people to keep their birthdays, as if they were glad that time was going away from them, people that don't use their time well either," moralised Halbert, looking earnestly in his mother's face, "and isn't new year's day just the same as a birthday and—" the boy hesitated and seemed unwilling or unable to say more.

"And what, Halbert," said Christian, as the boy paused and looked down, "and what—what was it you were going to say?"

"I don't know, Aunt Christian," hesitated Halbert, "I don't know whether it's right or not, but shouldn't we be rather sorry when the new year comes, than glad that the old year has ended?"

"And why sorry, Halbert?" said his father, who had hitherto been listening in silence, "why do you think we should be sorry?"

"Because, father," said Halbert, quickly, raising his eyes, "because you said in your sermon last Sabbath, that when once a year was gone, if we had not spent it well, it was entirely lost for ever, for we could never bring a minute back again."

"And therefore you think we should be sorry, do you, Halbert?" rejoined his father.

"Yes, father," was the answer, and again young Halbert's face was cast down, "for you say often that nobody spends their time well, or as right as they should do."

The elder Halbert did not answer, but he took little Christian, who had been gazing with her large eloquent eyes at every one that spoke in turn, and had attended diligently and earnestly to the unusual conversation, upon her aunt's knees. "Well, little one, do you think we should be sorry when the new year comes?"

"I think we should be both sorry and glad, papa," was the prompt answer.

"Well, Christian, Halbert has told us why we should be sorry; now do you tell us what it is we should be glad for."

There was a murmur among a little knot at a corner of the table, and a half-suppressed laugh before Christian had time to answer her father's question.

"Who is that? what is it that makes you so merry?" said Halbert, smiling and shaking his head at the merry urchins, who were congregated in a group.

"It's only our Halbert, uncle, it's only our Halbert," whispered little Mary Hamilton, deprecatingly.

"Well, Mary, we are impartial to-night, so we must hear what our Halbert has to say; come here, sir."

And Halbert Hamilton, the wildest little rogue that ever kept nursery in an uproar, or overcame nurse's patience, or conquered her heart by his feats of merry mischief, half hid himself below the table in pretended fear and dismay at his uncle's summons, and did not stir.

"Come, Halbert," said Mary, his mother, as Charles drew his incorrigible son into the middle of the little circle, "what did you say over there?"

Halbert the third looked down and blushed, and then laughed outright.

"He only said we should be glad when the new year comes, because we have plenty of *fun*," interposed Mary Melville, her wild cousin's constant defender and apologist.

"Quite right, my boy," said the elder Halbert, laying his hand kindly on the boy's head, "the coming of plenty of fun is a very good and proper thing to be glad for; but sit you down now, and let us hear what little Christian has to say." And Halbert sat down at his uncle's feet to listen.

"Well now, Christian, what should we be glad for? Is it because there is plenty of fun, as Halbert says?"

"No, papa," said the little, grave girl, seriously, shaking her head solemnly, "no, it is not that. I think it's because we have another to be good and do right in. Isn't that it, Aunt Christian?"

And the little girl looked over to her aunt inquiringly, to see if her childish conclusion was a correct one.

"Just so, my dear," was Aunt Christian's answer, as Halbert patted the child's soft cheek, and then permitted her to make her way over to her accustomed seat.

The children were gathered now about their parents' knees, and even wild Halbert Hamilton was silent and attentive. "Yes, children," said the kind father and uncle, as he looked round upon them, "yes, children, there is a better reason for being glad than even having plenty of fun. There is a new year to be good in, as little Christian says, a new year to live and learn in. It is true that, perhaps, you may not see its end; but, nevertheless, it is the beginning of a new year with many opportunities, both of doing and receiving good, and therefore we should be glad, and we *should* ask God to make us His faithful servants, loving Him and keeping His commandments all through this year, and if God does that you may be sure this will be a very happy new year to us all. Well, Halbert," he continued, turning to his son, who was back again by Aunt Christian's side, "has little Christian satisfied you?"

Halbert's face and conscience were both quite cleared; it was right to be glad on a new year's day, and he got a promise that that night he should hear some of the many things which had happened on former new years' days, and had made that day a special anniversary in the family; and besides, the relation of these things was to be committed to Aunt Christian, therefore Halbert was quite satisfied. And then the seniors closed round the fireside, and all the children—with the exception of Halbert Melville and Mary Hamilton, the eldest of the two families, who hang by Aunt Christian still—sought more active amusement in the farther corners of the room, and recollections of those bygone years became the long lingered on subject with Halbert, Charles, Christian, and the two Marys; and they looked back with half-wondering gaze upon the past, as men look through the wondrous glass of science on the clear outline of some far distant shore, of which the human dwellers, the fears and hopes, the loves and sorrows, which people the farther sides of the blue slopes that yet linger in their view, have all faded from their retiring vision.

But then comes a distant shout from the lobby into which some of the children have strayed in their play, of "Uncle James! Uncle James!" and here he is. Older, of course, yet looking much as he looked in the old times; though we must whisper that the bridegroom whom we saw some fourteen or fifteen years ago at the commencement of this story, has now, at its conclusion, become a portly gentleman; in good sooth, most unsentimentally *stout*, and with a look of comfort and competence about him, which speaks in tones most audibly, of worldly success and prosperity. A good man, too, and a pleasant, he is, with the milk of human kindness abounding in his heart; as such Mr. James Melville is universally considered and honoured, though with scarcely so large a heart as his brother the minister, nor so well mated. It is true, Mrs. James, since she found out who her friend of ten years ago was; and Mary's reasons for rejecting what seemed so good a match, and the failure, the utter failure of her party on that new year's night in consequence; has grown wonderfully careful, and begins to discover that there are pleasanter things in life, than the collecting together a dozen or two of people to be entertained or wearied according to their respective inclinations, and her fireside has grown a much more cheerful one always, though for a few nights in the year less brilliant than heretofore; and her husband's quotations of "Christian" have grown less disagreeable to her ears, though still she sometimes resents the superiority which everybody accords to her. James is always welcomed in his brother Halbert's house, and never more warmly than on New Year's night; for Elizabeth does not accompany him on these annual occasions; and even that loving circle feel relieved by her absence at such a time, for the conversation generally runs upon certain remembrances which she would not like to hear; and which none of them would like to mention in her presence. So James sits down and joins them for awhile in their recalling of the past; and little Halbert Melville gazes at his father in open-mouthed astonishment, as he hears him speak of being the cause of unhappiness and sorrow to Aunt Christian and Aunt Mary, and to Uncles James and Robert, and his grave old grandfather who died two years ago. His father—and Halbert would have defied anybody but that father's self. Yes! even Aunt Christian, if she had said such words as these—his father cause unhappiness and sorrow to anybody!—his father, whom old Ailie, still a hale and vigorous old woman, and chief of Christian's household, and prima donna in Mary Melville's nursery, had told him was always as kind and good to everybody all through his life as he was now! Halbert could not believe it possible. And little Mary Hamilton's eyes waxed larger and larger, in amazement, as Aunt Christian spoke of her mother—her mother whom she had never seen without a smile on her face, being at that infinitely remote period before any of them were born, most unhappy herself; yes, very unhappy! Mary would have denied it aloud, but that she had too much faith in Aunt Christian's infallibility, to doubt for an instant even her word. This night was a night of wonders to these two listening children.

But the time passed on, and Uncle James—while yet the other little ones were engaged in a merry game, chasing each other throughout all the house, from the glowing kitchen, clean and bright, up to the nursery where old Ailie presided in full state and glory—must go. Elizabeth was unwell; and he felt it was not seemly to be from home, loth and reluctant as he was to leave that fireside and its loving circle. So Uncle James prepared to go home; and down rushed again the whole merry band, deserted Ailie, even in the midst of one of her old-world stories, to bid him good-night; and thus environed by the little host with shouts as loud as had welcomed his arrival, Uncle James went away home.

CHAPTER II.

Men rail upon the Change!
*   *   *   *   *
But think they as they speak?
Thou softener of earth's pain,
Oh Change! sweet gift of the Infinite to the weak,
We hail alike thy sunshine and thy rain;
Awe dwells supreme in yon eternal light,
Horror in misery's doom;
But frail humanity dares breathe, when bright
Thy tremulous radiance mingles with the gloom.—Y.S.P.

UNCLE JAMES has just gone, and the group of elders in the parlour are just drawing their chairs closer together to fill up the gap which his departure has made, when they hear a hasty knock at the door; a hasty, imperative summons, as if from urgent need that would not be denied access, and a dripping messenger stands on the threshold—for the cold rain of winter falls heavily without—begging that Mr. Melville would go with him to see a dying man, a stranger who has taken up his residence for the last few weeks at a small inn in the neighbourhood, and was now, apparently, on the very brink of death, and in a dreadful state of mind. The calls of the sick and dying were as God's special commands to Halbert; and he rose at once to accompany the messenger, though the faces of his wife and sisters twain, darkened with care as he did so. It was very hard that he should be called away from them on this especial night; and when he firmly declared he would go, Mary whispered to Charles to go with him, and to bring him soon back. The two brothers went away through the storm, and the sisters drew closer to each other round the fire, as the gentlemen left them; then Mrs. Melville told the others how anxious she always was when her husband was called out in this way; how he might be exposed to infection in his visiting of the sick so assiduously as he did; and how, for his health's sake, she could almost wish he were less faithful and steady in the discharge of these his duties: and Mary looked at her in alarm as she spoke, and turned pale, and half upbraided herself for having unnecessarily exposed Charles, though a more generous feeling speedily suppressed her momentary selfishness. But Christian was by, and when was selfishness of thought, or an unbelieving fear harboured in Christian's gentle presence?

"Mary! Mary!" she exclaimed, as she turned from one to the other, "are you afraid to trust them in the hands of your Father? They are but doing what is their duty, and He will shield His own from all evil. Would you have your husband, Mary Melville, like these ministers whose whole work is their sermons—alas! there are many such—and who never try, whether visiting the sick and dying, or the vicious and criminal, would not advance their Master's cause as well—would you that, rather than Halbert's going forth as he has done to-night?"

"No, no; but it is terrible for me to think that he is exposed to all kinds of contagion; that he must go to fevers, and plagues, and diseases that I cannot name nor number, and run continually such fearful risks," said Mary, energetically.

"Our Father who is in Heaven, will protect him," said Christian, solemnly. "I have heard of a minister in London, who never for years ever thinks of seeing after his own people in their own homes; it is too much labour, forsooth, he is only their preacher, not their pastor; and though he sends—Reverend Doctor that he is—his deacons and such like to visit; it's seldom that himself ever goes to a poor sick bed, and as to his trying to reclaim the vicious, there is not on his individual part the least attempt or effort. Now, Mary, would you have Halbert such a man as that?"

"I would rather see him lying under the direfullest contagion. I would rather that he was stricken by the Lord's own hand, than that it should be said of Halbert Melville that he flinched in the least degree from the work which the Lord has laid upon him," returned Mary, proudly elevating her matronly form to its full height, with a dignity that gladdened Christian's heart.

"Yet that man in London will be well spoken of," said Mary Hamilton, "and our Halbert unknown. No matter: the time will come when Halbert will be acknowledged openly; and now, Christian, I feel assured and pleased that Charles went out with Halbert."

"And you may, when they went on such an errand," said Christian; "but"—and she continued briskly, as if to dispel the little gloom which had fallen upon them, and resuming the conversation, which had been broken off on the departure of the gentlemen—"but Robert writes me, that he is very comfortably settled, and likes his new residence well."

"I am sorry," said Mrs. Melville, after a pause, during which her agitation had gradually subsided, "I am sorry that I saw so little of Robert. He and I are almost strangers to each other."

"Not strangers, Mary, while so nearly connected," said Christian, kindly. "Moreover, Robert gives me several very intelligible hints about a young lady in your uncle's family to whom you introduced him."

"Indeed!" exclaimed Mrs. Melville, "no doubt he means my cousin Helen. Oh, I am very glad of that. Your brothers are too good, Christian, to be thrown away on cold-hearted, calculating people, who only look at money and money's worth——" and as the words fell from her lips, she stopped and blushed, and hesitated, for Mrs. James flashed upon her mind, and the comparison seemed invidious.

"You are quite right, Mary," said the other Mary, smiling; "and if Robert be as fortunate as Halbert has been, we shall be a happy family indeed."

Did Christian's brow grow dark with selfish sorrow, as she listened to these mutual congratulations? Nay, that had been a strange mood of Christian's mind in which self was uppermost, or indeed near the surface at all; and her whole soul rejoiced within her in sympathetic gladness. Nor, though they were happy in the full realisation of their early expectations, did she hold herself less blessed; for Christian bore about with her, in her heart of hearts, the holy memory of the dead, and in her hours of stillest solitude felt not herself alone. An angel voice breathed about her in whispering tenderness when she turned over the hallowed leaves of yon old Bible; and when the glorious light of sunset fell on her treasured picture, it seemed, in her glistening eyes, to light it up with smiles and gladness; and the time is gliding on gently and silently, day upon day falling like leaves in autumn, till the gates of yon far celestial city, gleaming through the mists of imperfect mortal vision, shall open to her humble footsteps, and the beloved of old welcome her to that everlasting reunion; and therefore can Christian rejoice, as well on her own account, as in ready sympathy with the joyful spirits round about her.

But the present evening wore gradually away, and the children became heavy, weary, and sleepy, and the youngest of all fairly fell asleep; and Mrs. Melville looked at her watch anxiously, and Mary said she could not wait for Charles, but must go home; but here again Christian interposed. The little Melvilles and Hamiltons had slept under the same roof before now, and being too far gone in weariness to have joined in their domestic worship, even had the elders been ready to engage in it, were taken off by twos and threes indiscriminately to their respective chambers; and the three sisters are left alone once more, maintaining, by fits and starts, a conversation that showed how their thoughts wandered; and, in this dreary interval of waiting for the home-coming of Halbert and Charles, listening to the doleful dropping of the slow rain without, until the long-continued suspense became intolerably painful. At length footsteps paused at the door; there was a knock, and some one entered, and each drew a long breath as if suddenly relieved, though Mrs. Melville started again, and became deadly pale, when Charles Hamilton entered the room alone. He seemed much agitated and distressed.

"Where is Halbert?" Mrs. Melville exclaimed; and her cry was echoed by the others at the fireside. "Has anything happened to Halbert?"

"Nothing—nothing: Halbert is quite well," said Charles, sitting down and wiping the perspiration from his forehead, while Halbert's wife clasped her hands in thankfulness. "He will be here soon; but I come from a most distressing scene—a deathbed—and that the deathbed of one who has spent his life as an infidel."

"A stranger, Charles?" asked Mary.

"A stranger, and yet no stranger to us," was Charles's answer; and he pressed his hands on his eyes, as though to shut out the remembrance of what he had so lately witnessed. As he spoke, the servants entered the room for the usual evening worship, under the impression that the master had returned; and Charles Hamilton took Halbert's place; and wife, and Christian, and the other Mary, marvelled when Charles's voice arose in prayer, at the earnest fervent tone of supplication with which he pleaded for that dying stranger, that the sins of his bygone life might not be remembered against him; and that the blood of atonement, shed for the vilest, might cleanse and purify that polluted soul, even in the departing hour; and to these listeners there seemed a something in Charles's prayer, as if the dying man and the sins of his fast fading life were thoroughly familiar to him and them.

A dreary journey it was for Halbert and Charles Hamilton as they left the warm social hearth and threaded the narrow streets in silence, following the sick man's messenger. It was a boisterous night, whose windy gusts whirled the heavy clouds along in quick succession, scattering them across the dark bosom of the sky, and anon embattling them in ponderous masses that lowered in apparent wrath over the gloomy world below. A strange contrast to the blithe house they had left was the clamour and rudeness of the obscure inn they entered now, and an unwonted visitor was a clergyman there; but up the narrow staircase were they led, and pausing for an instant on the landing-place, they listened for a moment to the deep groans and wild exclamations of impatient agony, as the sufferer tossed about on his uneasy bed.

"Ay, sir," said a servant, who came out of the room with a scared and terrified expression upon her face, in answer to Halbert's inquiry; "ay, sir, he's very bad; but the worst of it is not in his body, neither!" and she shook her head mysteriously; "for sure he's been a bad man, and he's a deal on his mind."

She held open the door as she said so, and the visitors entered. The scanty hangings of his bed hid them from the miserable man who lay writhing and struggling there, and the brothers started in utter amazement as they looked upon the wasted and dying occupant of that poor room; the brilliant, the fashionable, the rich, the talented Forsyth—where were all these vain distinctions now?—lay before them, labouring in the last great conflict; poor, deserted, forlorn, and helpless, without a friend, without a hope, with scarce sufficient wealth to buy the cold civility of the terrified nurse who tended him with mercenary carelessness; pressing fast into the wide gloom of eternity, without one feeble ray of life or hope to guide him on that fearful passage, or assuage the burning misery of his soul ere it set out. Halbert Melville, deceived by that poor sufferer of old, bent down his face on his clasped hands, speechless, as the well-known name trembled on his companion's tongue,—

"Forsyth!"

"Who calls me?" said the dying man, raising himself fearfully on his skeleton arm, and gazing with his fiery sunken eyes through the small apartment. "Who spoke to me? Hence!" he exclaimed, wildly sitting up erect and strong in delirious fury. "Hence, ye vile spirits! Do I not come to your place of misery? Why will ye torment me before my time?"

His trembling attendant tried to calm him: "A minister," she said, "had come to see him." He said: "*He* allow a minister to come and speak with him?"

A wild laugh was the response. "To speak with *me*, me that am already in torment! Well, let him come," he said, sinking back with a half-idiotic smile, "let him come"—— and he muttered the conclusion of the sentence to himself.

"Will you come forward, sir?" said the nurse, respectfully addressing Halbert. "He is composed now."

Trembling with agitation, Halbert drew nearer the bedside, but when those burning eyes, wandering hither and thither about the room, rested on him, a maniac scream rang through the narrow walls, and the gaunt form sat erect again for a moment, with its long arms lifted above its head, and then fell back in a faint, and Halbert Melville hung over his ancient deceiver as anxiously as though he had been, or deserved in all respects to be, his best beloved; and when the miserable man awoke to consciousness again, the first object his eye fell upon, was Halbert kneeling by his bedside, chafing in his own the cold damp hand of Forsyth, with kindest pity pictured on his face. Had Halbert disdained him, had he shunned or reproached him, poor Forsyth, in the delirious strength of his disease, would have given him back scorn for scorn, reproach for reproach. But, lo! the face of this man, whom he had wounded so bitterly, was beaming on him now in compassion's gentlest guise; and the fierce despairing spirit melted like a child's, and the dying sinner wept.

"Keep back, Charles!" whispered Halbert, as he rose from the bedside; "the sight of you might awaken darker feelings, and he seems subdued and softened now. There may yet be hope."

Hope!—the echo of that blessed word has surely reached the quick ear of the sufferer; and it draws from him a painful moan and bitter repetition as he turns his weary form on his couch again: "Hope! who speaks of hope to me?"

"I do," said Halbert Melville, mildly looking upon the ghastly face whose eyes of supernatural brightness were again fixed upon him. "I do, Forsyth; I, who have sinned as deeply, and in some degree after the same fashion as you. I am commissioned to speak of hope to all—of hope, even on the brink of the grave—of hope to the chief of sinners. Yes, I am sent to speak of hope," he continued, growing more and more fervent, while the sick man's fascinated attention and glowing eyes followed each word he uttered and each motion of his lifted hand. "Yes, of hope a thousand times higher in its faintest aspirations than the loftiest ambition of the world."

"Ay, Melville," he murmured, feebly overcome by his weakness and emotion. "Ay, but not for me, not for one like me. Why do you come here to mock me?" he added fiercely, after a momentary pause; "why do you come here to insult me with your offers of hope? I am beyond its reach. Let me alone; there is no hope, no help for me!" and again his voice sunk into feebleness, as he murmured over and over these despairing words, like, Charles Hamilton said afterwards, the prolonged wail of a lost soul.

"Listen to me, Forsyth," said Halbert, seating himself by the bedside, and bending over the sufferer. "Listen to me! You remember how *I* denied my God and glorified in the denial when last I saw you. You remember how *I* renounced my faith and hope," and Halbert, pale with sudden recollection, wiped the cold perspiration from his forehead. "You know, likewise, how I left my home in despair—such despair as you experience now. Listen to me, Forsyth, while I tell you how I regained hope."

Forsyth groaned and hid his face in his hands, for Halbert had touched a chord in his heart, and a flood of memories rushed back to daunt and confound him, if that were possible, still more and more; and then, for there seemed something in Halbert's face that fascinated his burning eyes, he turned round again to listen, while Halbert began the fearful story of his own despair—terrible to hear of—terrible to tell; but, oh! how much more terrible to remember, as what oneself has passed through. With increasing earnestness as he went on, the poor sufferer gazed and listened, and at every pause a low moan, wrung from his very soul, attested the fearful faithfulness of the portraiture, true in its minutest points. It was a sore task for Halbert Melville to live over again, even in remembrance, those awful years, and exhibit the bygone fever of his life for the healing of that wounded soul; but bravely did he do it, sparing not the pain of his own shrinking recollection, but unfolding bit by bit the agonies of his then hopelessness, so fearfully reproduced before him now in this trembling spirit, till Charles, sitting unseen in a corner of the small apartment, felt a thrill of awe creep over him, as he listened and trembled in very sympathy; but when Halbert's voice, full of saddest solemnity, began to soften as he spoke of hope, of that hope that came upon his seared heart like the sweet drops of April rain, reviving what was desolate, of hope whose every smile was full of truthfulness, and certainty, firmer than the foundations of the earth, more enduring than the blue sky or the starry worlds above, built upon the divine righteousness of Him who died for sinners;—the heart of the despairing man grew sick within him, as though the momentary gleam which irradiated his hollow eye was too precious, too joyful, to abide with him in his misery—and, lo! the hardened, obdurate, and unbelieving spirit was struck with the rod of One mightier than Moses, and hiding his pale face on his tear-wet pillow, the penitent man was ready to sob with the Prophet, "Oh! that mine head were waters, and mine eyes a fountain of tears!"

A solemn stillness fell upon that sick-room when Halbert's eloquent tale was told; a stillness that thrilled them as though it betokened the presence of a visitor more powerful than they. The solitary light by the bedside fell upon the recumbent figure, with its thin arms stretched upon the pillow, and its white and ghastly face hidden thereon—full upon the clasped hands of God's generous servant, wrestling in silent supplication for that poor helpless one. It was a solemn moment, and who may prophesy the issue, the end of all this? A little period passed away, and the fever of the sick man's despair was assuaged, and weariness stole over his weak frame, with which his fiery rage of mind had hitherto done battle; and gentle sleep, such as had never refreshed his feeble body since he lay down on this bed, closed those poor eyelids now. Pleasant to look upon was that wasted face, in comparison with what it was when Halbert Melville saw its haggard features first of all this night. God grant a blessed awakening.

Softly Halbert stole across the room, and bade Charles go; as soon as he could leave Forsyth he promised that he would return home, but it might be long ere he could do that, and he called the nurse, who was waiting without the door, to see how her patient slept. She looked at him in amazement. Nor was the wonder less of the doctor, who came almost immediately after—he could not have deemed such a thing possible, and if it continued long, it yet might save his life, spent and wasted as he was; but he must still be kept in perfect quietness. Halbert took his station at the bedside as the doctor and nurse left the room, and shading Forsyth's face with the thin curtain, he leant back, and gave himself up for a time to the strange whirl of excited feeling which followed. The memories so long buried, so suddenly and powerfully awakened; the image of this man, as he once was, and what he was now. Compassion, interest, hope, all circled about that slumbering figure, till Halbert's anxiety found vent in its accustomed channel, prayer. The night wore slowly on, hour after hour pealed from neighbouring clocks till the chill grey dawn of morn crept into the sick-room, making the solitary watcher shiver with its breath of piercing cold; and not until the morning was advanced, till smoke floated over every roof, and the bustle of daily life had begun once more, did the poor slumberer awake. Wonderingly, as he opened his eyes, did he gaze on Halbert: wonderingly and wistfully, as the events of the past night came up before him in confused recollections, and he perceived that Halbert, who bent over him with enquiries, had watched by his side all night. Forsyth shaded his eyes with his thin hand, and murmured a half weeping acknowledgment of thankfulness, "This from you, Melville, this from you!"

CHAPTER III.

Hope the befriending,
Does what she can, for she points evermore up to heaven, and faithful
Plunges her anchor's peak in the depths of the grave, and beneath it
Paints a more beautiful world * * * *
 * * * Then praise we our Father in Heaven,
Him, who has given us more; for to us has Hope been illumined;
Groping no longer in night; she is Faith, she is living assurance;
Faith is enlighten'd hope; she is light, is the eye of affection;
Dreams of the longing interprets, and carves their visions in marble;
Faith is the sun of life; and her countenance shines like the Prophet's,
For she has look'd upon God.—EVANGELINE.

THERE were anxious enquiries mingling with the glad welcome which Halbert Melville received as he entered his own house on that clear cold winter's morning,—for the evening's rain had passed away, and frost had set in once more—enquiries that showed the interest which both his own Mary and Christian—for Christian's society, though she did not allow it to be monopolised by either, was claimed in part by both the Marys, and her time divided between them—felt in the unhappy sufferer.

"Does Mary know, Christian?" was one of Halbert's first questions.

"Yes," was the answer, "and much was she shocked and grieved, of course; as was Charles also, but we were all rejoiced to hear from him that a happy influence seemed at work before he left you. Has it gone on? Can he see any light yet, Halbert?"

"I dare not answer you, Christian," said her brother gravely. "I know too well the nature of Forsyth's feelings to expect that he should speedily have entire rest; but God has different ways of working with different individuals, and I have reason to give Him thanks for my own terrible experience, as I believe my account of it was the means of softening the heart of yon poor despairing man."

"How wonderful, Halbert," said Christian, laying her hand on his shoulder; "how wonderful are the ways and workings of Providence. Who could have imagined that you were to be the instrument, as I trust and pray you may be, of turning your old tempter from the evil of his ways, and leading him into the way of salvation!"

A month of the new year glided rapidly away, when one mild Sabbath morning, a thin pale man, prematurely aged, entered Halbert Melville's church. The exertion of walking seemed very great and painful to him, and he tottered, even though leaning on his staff, as he passed along to a seat. A sickly hue was still upon his wasted features, and the hair that shaded his high forehead was white, apparently more from sorrow than from years. When he had seated himself, he cast around him a humble wistful glance, as though he felt himself alone and begged for sympathy; and people of kindly nature who took their places near him, felt themselves powerfully drawn to the lonely stranger who looked so pale, and weak, and humble, and wondered who he was; and many of them who watched him with involuntary interest, noticed the quick flush that passed over his face as Mary Hamilton entered, and how he gazed upon the other Mary, and lingered with glistening eyes on every little one of the two smiling families, as though their childish grace rejoiced his heart; but the observers wondered still more when their minister had entered the pulpit to see the big round tears which fell silently upon the stranger's open Bible, and the expression of almost womanly tenderness that shone in every line of his upturned face. Mr. Melville, they said afterwards, was like a man inspired that day—so clear, so full, so powerful was his sermon. His text was in one of Isaiah's sublime prophecies. "Look unto me and be ye saved, all the ends of the earth, for I am God, and besides me there is none else." And as he drew with rapid pencil the glorious character of the divine speaker, in all the majesty of the original Godhead, and also of his Mediatorial glory, his hearers felt that he that day spoke like one inspired. Vividly he described them lost in natural darkness, groping about the walls of their prison-house, labouring to grasp the meteor light which flitted hither and thither about each earthly boundary, hopeless and helpless, when this voice rang through the gloom, "Look unto me and be ye saved." Vividly he pictured the entering light, which to the saved followed these words of mercy, steady, unfailing, and eternal, that sprung from point to point of these desolate spirit cells, illuminating the walls with heavenly radiance, and making them prisons no longer, but changing them into temples dedicate to the worship of the highest. "My brethren," said the eloquent preacher, bending down in his earnestness, as though he would speak to each individual ere he concluded. "There are those among you who know the blessedness of being thus plucked from the everlasting burnings—there are among you those who have worn out years in a fiery struggle before they found rest;" and the voice of the preacher trembled; "and there are those whose anguish has been compressed into a little round of days; but I know also that there are some here who can echo the words of one who knew in his own dread experience the agony of despair:

"'I was a stricken deer that left the herd
Long since, with many an arrow deep infixed
My panting sides were charged;'

and I rejoice to know that here there are those who can continue in the same words—

"'There 'twas I met One who had himself
Been hit by the archers, in his hands he bore
And in his pierced side, their cruel wounds;
With gentle force soliciting the darts,
He drew them out, and heal'd, and bade me live.'

and, oh, my brethren, did you but know the fearful suffering, the hopeless anguish that follows a course of lost opportunities and despised mercies, you would not need that I should bid you flee! escape for your lives, tarry not in the cell, the plain fair and well watered, and like the garden of the Lord though it seem; escape to the mountain lest ye be consumed. 'Look unto me and be ye saved, all the ends of the earth, for I am God, and besides me there is none else.'"

The face of the lonely stranger is hidden, but those who sit near him are turning round in wonder at the echoing sob which bore witness to the effect of these thrilling words upon his mind; but when the minister had closed his book, and the people united their voices in praise before the service ended, the weak low accents of that humble man were heard mingling among them, for he had found *hope*, even such hope and peace as the preacher of this day had proclaimed in yonder dim sick-chamber to its dying occupant; and this lowly man was he, raised as by a miracle at once from the gates of hell, and from the brink of the grave. With gentle sympathy did Halbert Melville, his work of mercy over, press the hand of that grateful man; with kindly anticipation of his unexpressed wish did he bring the children one by one before him, and they wondered in their happy youthfulness as the hand of that slender stooping figure trembled on each graceful head; and when the two little Marys hand in hand came smiling up Forsyth did not ask their names. He discovered too clearly the resemblance shining in the daughter, and scarce less distant in the niece of Mary Melville of old, and he murmured blessings upon them. He feared to hear the name which brought so many painful recollections in its sweet and pleasant sound.

But when a little time had passed away, Forsyth learned to love the very shadow of Mary Melville's eldest born, and cherished her as she sprang up in graceful girlhood, as though she had been the child of his own old age, the daughter of his heart. The solitary stranger was soon better known to the hearers of the Rev. Halbert Melville, for he lingered about the place as though its very stones were dear to him. Forsyth had made no friends in his long season of sinful wealth and prosperity—gay acquaintances he had had in plenty who joined his guiltiness, and called themselves friends, until the new course of folly and excess on which he entered with headlong avidity after Mary Melville rejected him, had dissipated his substance and made him poor, and then the forlorn sufferer in his obscure apartment found out the true value of these his heartless companions' friendship. But now, a new man among friends on whose unworldly sincerity he could rely without a shadow of a doubt, his very worldly prospects brightened, and gathering the remnants of his broken fortunes, he began now to use the remainder of God's once abundant gifts with a holy prudence, that made his small substance more valuable a thousand fold, than the larger income that had been so lavishly expended in the long years of his guilt and darkness; a changed man was he in every particular, the talent which made him foremost in the ranks of infidelity was laid upon God's altar now, a consecrated thing, and men who knew him first after his great changes, marvelled at his strange humility, so unlike the world in its simple lowliness. When he was told of the sinful and erring he bent his head and blamed them not, for the remembrance of his own sins filled him with gentlest charity, and when deed of mercy was to be done, that needed earnest exertion and zealous heart, the mild and gentle Forsyth was ever foremost delighting in the labour.

The threads of our tale have nearly run out; and we have but, as knitters say, to take them up ere we finish. Our Halbert Melville is famed and honoured; a wise and earnest minister, faithful and fervent in his pulpit, unwearying in daily labour. His gentle Mary becomes the sweet dignity of her matronhood well, rejoicing in the happy guardianship of these fair children. Nor is the other Mary less blessed: the liberal heavens have rained down gifts upon them all; seed-time and harvest, summer and winter, have passed over their heads; but death and sorrow, making sad visits to many homes around them, and leaving havoc and desolation in their train, have never in their stern companionship come across these peaceful thresholds. Now we must draw the veil, lest we should feel the hot breath of sickness in these happy households, or see the approaching shadow of grief darkening their pleasant doorways.

Our friend James grows rich apace; and were you to see his portly figure and shining face "on Change," where merchants most do congregate, you would be at no loss to understand why his opinion is now so weighty and influential. Messrs. Rutherford and Melville left a goodly beginning for their more enterprising successor; and James is now a most prosperous, because a most enterprising man. Robert, too, though at a distance in another city, the resident partner of his brother's great house, speeds well in his vocation; and wedding one of his gentle sister-in-law's kindred, has made up our tale. The Melvilles are truly, as Mary said, a happy family.

But how shall we say farewell to our companion of so many days and various vicissitudes—our generous single-minded Christian Melville; fain would we linger over every incident of thy remaining story. Fain look upon thee once more, dear Christian, in the sacred quietness of thine own chamber, recalling the holy memories of the past. Fain go with thee through thy round of duties, rejoicing in the love which meets thy gracious presence everywhere. Fain would we add to our brief history another tale, recording how the stubborn resolutions of a second Halbert would yield to no persuasions less gentle than thine; and how the guileless hearts of the twain Marys unfolded their most secret thinkings in sweetest confidence to only thee; how thou wert cherished, and honoured, and beloved, dear Christian; how willingly would we tell, how glad look forward through the dim future, to prophesy thee years of happiness as bright and unclouded as this, and testify to the truth of that old saying of Halbert's, "that Christian would never grow old." But now we must bid thee farewell, knowing how "thy soul, like a quiet palmer, travellest unto the land of heaven;" and believing well that, Christian, whatever may happen to thee in thy forward journey, however it may savour now, be it fresh trials or increased joys, will work nothing but final good and pleasantness to thy subdued and heavenly spirit—has not our Father said that all things shall work together for good to them that love God as thou dost?—bringing but a more abundant entrance at thy latter days into the high inheritance in thy Father's Kingdom, which waits for the ending of thy pilgrimage, dear Christian Melville.

THE END.

———

www.ingramcontent.com/pod-product-compliance
Ingram Content Group UK Ltd.
Pitfield, Milton Keynes, MK11 3LW, UK
UKHW031338260325
456749UK00002B/345